This book is dedicated to my son, Bill, who makes me proud every day; my wonderful wife, Denise, who believes in me more than I deserve, and to my beautiful daughters, Emma and Rachel, who may never understand this world, but allow me to share in theirs.

My sincere thanks to Karen Syed at Echelon Press for taking a chance on me; Jenny Turner for her excellent editorial input; Nathalie Moore of Graphics Muse for producing such fantastic cover art; Lew Preschel, Jim (J.J.) Lair, Cole DeNardo, Bill Mingin, Andrew Alford and Cherry Weiner for their invaluable critique and feedback on early drafts, as well as all my other friends at The Garden State Horror Writers, The Greater Lehigh Valley Writers Group, The Monmouth Creative Writing Group, The WritersCoffeehouseOnline Yahoo Group and on Live Journal for their encouragement and support.

Chapter One
A Change of Plan

Getting it back would be dangerous. Snowy would have to return tomorrow, and that meant avoiding Razor for one more night.

He decided to risk it, hiding out in the stables behind Daft Aggie's place, where the stench of horse manure and urine-soaked hay masked his scent. Hungry and miserable, he didn't dare show his face. Razor was out there somewhere, watching, waiting.

At dawn, he crept past the sleeping horses into the fresh air, then set off through the village, keeping an eye out for any sign of pursuit. By the time he passed the old church, the sun had risen. To his near colorblind eyes, it hung in the air like a plate of molten silver, casting its benevolent glow over the village of Little Chumberry.

When he reached Mrs. Willikin's cottage, he hauled himself over the low stone wall in front, then made his way along the side. At the far end, he poked his head around the corner, closing his mouth to avoid the overpowering smell from the flowers which smothered most of the back yard.

Keeping his head low, he scurried across the grass to hide amongst the rose bushes.

Despite the grumbles from his empty belly, he allowed himself a smile. When the new owners arrived, he'd sneak inside, retrieve his prized possession, and be on his way. By nightfall, he'd be miles from the village. With any luck, Razor would never find him.

A cruel voice called out from the bottom of the garden. "Hello, Snowy."

At the sound of his name, Snowy let out something between a scream and a hiss. He jumped six inches off the ground, turning in mid-air to land facing Razor, who stepped out from behind the garden shed.

Looking less than happy, Razor trotted up the garden path. Sunlight reflected off the peculiar metal helmet on his head. "Haven't heard from you in three days. I hope you aren't planning to run out on me. You enjoy my protection now, but try to leave before the job's done and I'll tear you inside out."

Snowy backed away, wary of the prickly thorns behind him, but all too conscious of the sharp teeth and claws on the animal in front. "I need more time."

"You've had plenty. You were supposed to find a human to help me, but all I ever see you do is beg them for food."

"I don't beg. I just let them feed me sometimes… when I'm starving…or hungry…or feeling a bit peckish."

Razor paced up and down on the grass verge. "Fur-Face took my family. I need a human to get them back."

"I know, but it's not that easy. Look, I speak their language, we both do, but none of the humans I've approached can hear me. What if I can't find anyone?"

"That would be unfortunate…for you." In a blur of motion, Razor bit the head off the nearest rose and spat it into the air. The torn petals gave off a bittersweet fragrance as they spiraled to the ground.

Razor leaped onto the water barrel by the shed door, then looked back over his shoulder. "Remember, I can find your trail as easily as a bird finds the sky. Don't disappoint me." Without waiting for an answer, he jumped over the wall.

Snowy pawed at the ground.

I'm shredded either way. I've tried every human in the village. None of them can hear me. No, don't think like that. Keep your nerve. When the new owners arrive, nip inside, get it back, then head out across the fields toward the theme park. What with all those stale car fumes from the main road, even Razor won't be able to pick up your scent.

His ears pricked up. There it was again, a faint rustling sound, coming from beneath a nearby shrubbery. He saw movement from the corner of his eye, then pounced. After a short while, he returned to the rose bush, still thirsty, but no longer hungry.

At midday, a car and a small van pulled up in front of the cottage. Snowy trotted over to investigate. Out of sight of the newcomers, he crept along the base of the low wall separating the front yard from the road. As he reached the gate, a woman pushed it open. She hurried up the path, rummaging through her handbag as she went.

Snowy followed. At the front door, the woman had trouble with the lock. He sat on the path behind her, his tail twitching. "Get a move on, love. I haven't got all day."

Oblivious to the impatient cat at her heels, the

woman pulled out another key.

"Move yourself, furball." A man tottered up the garden path behind Snowy, his legs buckling beneath the weight of the huge bundle on his back. Not wishing to be flattened, Snowy scampered off the path.

"Where do you want this carpet, Mrs. Euston?"

"Upstairs, on the landing," the woman said. "That is, if I can ever get us inside."

She put her shoulder to the door. It flew open, but Snowy didn't dare approach now, for fear of getting trampled on.

"We moved the bedroom furniture in last night," Mrs. Euston said. "My husband's due here in a couple of hours with the children and the rest of our things. Will you have finished by then?"

Snowy didn't hear the reply, because she closed the front door. He clawed at the welcome mat. *Last night! I don't believe it. If I'd have just stayed here, I could have got in then.*

An awful thought struck him. *What if they took it?* He banished the idea from his mind. What would humans want with an old chew toy? Hell, most cats wouldn't even give it a second glance, but it was all he had left to remind him of her, and to get it back, he'd risk anything, even Razor's sharp teeth.

A drop of water splashed on his whiskers.

Another fell, and another. He scurried across the grass to shelter beneath the apple tree in the middle of the front lawn.

When the workmen left, he made another attempt to get in the house, but Mrs. Euston shooed him away. Damp and dejected, he went back to the tree and scrambled onto the lowest branch to wait for a better opportunity.

By the time the rest of the family's belongings arrived, the sun had come out again. A taxi pulled up behind the removal truck. A nervous-looking boy got out, followed by a man carrying a little girl. The toddler squealed with delight when she saw her new home.

The boy seemed less enthusiastic. As they walked up the garden path he held out a cell phone to show his father. "No signal. I knew it."

Snowy loitered near the front door. Several times, he managed to walk in behind one of the laborers as they carried a seemingly endless procession of cardboard boxes inside the house, but someone always chased him out before he reached the stairs.

Just when he began to think he might never get inside, his chance came. As the removal men maneuvered a fridge-freezer through the kitchen doorway, one of them knocked a packing box off the table. It hit the ground with an expensive crash, spewing broken china across the tiled floor.

While the humans scrambled to clear up the mess, Snowy dashed through the front doorway.

The house reeked of new carpet. Even with his mouth closed, the smell of it all but took his breath away. He scampered up the stairs, keeping to the wall where no one could spot him from the kitchen, but when he reached the landing, he snagged his front, right paw in the lush, bottle-green carpet.

He tried to pull free, without success.

Another tug, harder this time. A few inches of thread unraveled. He rolled over and over in an effort to twist free. If anything, it made things worse.

Standing on three legs, facing the staircase, Snowy examined the mesh of green fabric around his claws and paw. *How did it get so tangled?*

Someone flushed the toilet in the upstairs bathroom behind him.

Frantic now, he scratched and clawed at the twined threads tethering him to the landing. The frayed edges billowed like candy floss, but held firm. At the sound of running water he redoubled his efforts, this time using his teeth.

The door opened.

The children's father backed out of the bathroom, waving a can of air freshener about him. Snowy gave a last, desperate heave. The thread snapped. He scampered to the bedroom at the far end of the landing as a cloud of lavender mist descended behind him. He charged through the open doorway, then dived sideways to hide beneath the twin bed which had not been there the last time he'd been in the room.

The boy sat slouched over a desk by the window, staring off into the horizon. The little girl lay on the bed, watching TV with the sound off.

From his hiding place, Snowy listened for signs of pursuit.

Nothing.

On the day he'd returned to the cottage to find himself locked out, he'd left his keepsake in the built-in closet on the far wall, along with Mrs. Willikin's TV remote and a half-eaten candy bar. The closet door was closed now. He could open it, but not without the children seeing him. Can't risk getting caught, he decided.

If they chuck me out again, I might never get back inside. I'll wait till things settle down. Once I get it back, I'll hide out until someone opens the front door, then scarper.

He curled into a ball and tried to settle down, but a strange sound came from by the window, like blunt claws scratching on a smooth surface.

Curious, Snowy crawled forward to see what made the noise. The boy huddled over his desk, with a colored pencil in his hand.

An artist. No wonder he looks so bloomin' miserable.

He crawled back out of sight. Despite the unfamiliar smells and constant noise, he soon fell asleep.

Some time later, he woke with a start to find night had fallen. He could hear slow breathing coming from the bed above. Otherwise, aside from a soothing tick…tock…tick…tock from somewhere downstairs, the house stood in complete silence.

Not quite how I planned it, he thought, but the same result.

He crept out from his hiding place.

It was time.

Chapter Two
Things That go 'Burp' in the Night

Thirteen years old, short for his age and slightly built, Billy Euston had felt out of place among the classmates he'd left behind in London, who'd all sprung up like high-rise apartment blocks during the previous year. The nagging worry that his long-overdue growth spurt was not late, but had, in fact, passed him by altogether, gnawed constantly at his already well-chewed self-esteem.

He had loving parents, a good home, but few friends. When not at school, he spent most of his time in his bedroom, working on *The Adventures of Static-Man*, a comic book he'd conceived and was attempting to produce by himself.

In the run-up to the family's relocation from London to Little Chumberry, Billy had become even more of a recluse. He knew his parents worried about their son's imaginative nightmares and the ever-anxious expression on his face. A look he wore now, on his first night in their new home, as he sat up in bed and stared into the darkness.

"Is someone there?"

The scuffling sound from inside his bedroom closet stopped, but there was no reply.

Billy let out a deep sigh. His father had warned him

about this. After thirteen years of living in London, their new home would be filled with unfamiliar noises, especially at night. He took a nervous gulp of water from the glass at his bedside table, then lay back down, grateful the summer holidays had started. If he ever did get to sleep, at least he wouldn't have to get up early tomorrow.

The scuffling noise started again.

He tried to relax, but it was no use. Now he imagined a strange voice, muttering to itself.

"Where is it?" the voice asked. "Must be in here somewhere. Maybe they put it on the shelf...oops!"

Something landed on the closet floor with a muffled 'thump'.

Billy sat bolt upright. This was not his imagination. With his heart wedged in his throat, he slid out of bed. As he tiptoed across the floor, an unpleasant gurgling came from inside the closet, followed by a loud belch.

With a terrified shriek he dashed out of the room, slamming the door behind him, then raced down the hall, where he collided with his father.

"What's wrong, son?"

"Someone's in my room."

Dr. Euston rolled his eyes. "I thought we talked about this. All right, let's take a look." He marched down the hall and made a great show of pushing open the bedroom door. "We know you're in there." He switched on the light. "Come out quietly, or there'll be trouble."

No one answered.

Dr. Euston stepped inside.

Billy heard a door open, then his father's voice. "Hello, little fellow. How did you get in here?"

He looked into his room to see his father holding what looked like an overstuffed, black, velvet cushion.

"It's just the cat from yesterday, son. Remember how it kept hanging around in the front yard while the removal men unloaded our stuff? It must have been nosing about inside and gone to sleep in your room."

Billy stared, dumbfounded, into the closet. His collection of superhero bubblegum cards lay scattered across the floor beside the box in which he kept them.

Just then, his mother appeared in the bedroom doorway, carrying his two-year-old sister, Emma. "Everything all right, Jim?"

His father glanced at the digital clock on the bedside table. "It's nothing, Louise, just a cat." He grinned at Billy. "I hope your scream didn't wake the neighbors. They'll think there's been a murder or something. You certainly gave me a fright."

While Billy's mother took Emma back to her room, his father sat on the bed. He let go of the cat, which paced up and down on the covers behind him, rubbing itself against his back each time it passed.

Billy couldn't think what to say. The initial relief he felt had gone, elbowed aside by humiliation and embarrassment. "I'm so sorry, Dad. I heard something in the closet. I could swear it spoke. It was looking for something."

The cat paused for a moment to give him a curious look, then continued pacing.

"It's all right, son. I understand." Dr. Euston gestured around the room at the homemade posters pinned on the walls. Most of them pictures of Static-man. "You have a fantastic imagination. That's a good thing, of course. I just wish you could learn to switch it off when you go to bed. Still, I suppose a talking cat is a step up from the giant octopus you dreamed about the other night."

"I know. I'm sorry. I feel like such an idiot."

The cat settled on the bed, massaging the pillow with its front paws before curling into a sleeping position.

Billy stroked its head. "Stupid cat, you made me look like a right twit."

It stared back at him. "You can't blame me for that, mate, I'm not the one who screamed like a little girl."

Billy fainted.

When he came to, he opened his eyes to see his mother staring at him with an anxious expression. "How are you feeling?"

"Where is it?" he asked, painfully aware of the tremble in his voice. He sat up.

"Your father took it into the back garden. Why are you suddenly afraid of cats?"

"I'm not. It just took me by surprise when it talked, that's all."

She looked away.

"Dad heard it too, ask him."

"I'll…get you some warm milk."

Billy opened his mouth to protest, but realized how insane he must sound. His mother brought him the milk, and sat with him until he'd drunk it all. "Try to get some sleep. You'll feel better in the morning."

An hour later, Billy threw back the bedcovers. "I am not going crazy," he announced, to the empty room. At the window, he pulled the curtains behind his head. The glass felt cool against his nose.

The cat stared at him from the middle of the back yard.

It's waiting for me.

He pulled on his dressing gown and slippers, then tiptoed down the hall. As he passed the open door of his parents' bedroom he folded his arms, tight across his chest, worried the thunderous beating of his heart would wake everyone, but no one stirred. Once in the kitchen, he closed the door behind him, then fumbled for the light switch.

The sudden brightness blinded him. On the other side of the window, the garden seemed much darker, but he could still make out the cat's outline.

It hadn't moved.

He eased open the back door. In a loud whisper, he said, "Cooeee, here kitty."

Nothing happened.

Billy tried again, this time puckering his lips to make kissing noises. "Here kitty-kitty. Here kitty-kitty-kitty."

The cat didn't budge.

He took a deep breath, then stepped outside into the warm, night air.

The cat watched as he crouched down and shuffled toward it, clicking his fingers. "C'mon boy, here kitty-kitty."

When he got within a few feet, the cat spoke. "What on earth are you doing?"

"You *can* talk, I knew it." Billy felt too happy to find he wasn't going crazy to be scared anymore.

"That's hardly a surprise. I spoke to you earlier didn't I? A regular little Einstein, you are. By the way, good idea, pretending to faint so your dad wouldn't get suspicious. Quick thinking, kid. Well done."

It paced the grass in front of him. He felt its paws through the tops of his slippers when it stepped on his feet.

"So what's with all the 'Here, kitty-kitty' stuff?"

"I was trying to get your attention." With eyes now fully accustomed to the moonlight, Billy became all too aware of the cat's blank stare. His cheeks flushed hot and he began to shiver. It wasn't a cold night, but he suddenly wanted to be inside.

"You know: 'Here kitty-kitty'?"

The cat wagged a paw at him. "That's stereotyping that is. Just 'cause I'm a cat, doesn't mean I should come running any time a human clicks his fingers or sloshes a bowl of milk in my direction."

Billy mumbled an apology. "Sorry. I wasn't thinking. My dad's a vet, but I'm not used to animals."

"All right, we'll let it go this time. By the way," the cat rubbed against his shins, "*have* you got any milk?"

A few minutes later, Billy sat at the kitchen table, watching, wide-eyed, as the cat finished off a second helping.

"What's the matter with you? Never seen a cat drink milk before?"

"Of course I have..." He paused as the cat sucked the last drops of milk from the bottom of the glass with a loud slurping noise, "But I've never seen one use a bendy straw."

The cat grinned. "Nice bit of dairy that. You can't

beat a drop of the old full-cream. Unless, of course, you have any cola."

Billy ignored the hint. "What were you looking for in my room?"

"Your room? Until this morning it was mine."

"This cottage stood empty for weeks before we moved in. Nobody lived here."

"I did," the cat said. "I used to come here all the time before old Mrs. Willikin emigrated. Treated me like one of the family she did. We watched the telly together most evenings. I moved in permanent after she left. She always had a snack and a bit of milk for a starving cat like myself."

"Starving?" Billy glanced at the cat's more than ample belly, but decided not to argue the point. "Mom had professional cleaners go over the whole house yesterday. I'm afraid whatever you left there would have been thrown out." The cat seemed to deflate in front of him. "I'm sorry. Was it valuable?"

"Only to me."

They sat in uncomfortable silence. After a while, the cat let out a heavy sigh. "I suppose tonight wasn't a total loss," it muttered, more to itself than to Billy. "I've found a human who can hear me. That should get him off my back." It let out a loud belch. "Pardon me. Still, better out than in. Now then, I expect you're wondering how I'm able to talk."

"Not in the least. I already know."

"You do?"

"Yes, I should have realized it earlier. This is a dream. Normal rules don't apply when you're dreaming. Anything can happen. I even had one about flying cows once."

The cat tilted its head to one side. "I don't feel like a dream." It stepped across the table toward him. "If I'm not real, why did you come and get me from the garden?"

"I didn't. As a matter of fact, I'm upstairs in my bed. I told you, I'm still asleep. I'll just go along with whatever's happening, then I'll wake up and it'll be morning– Ouch!"

Billy grabbed a paper towel to soak up the thin line of blood which oozed from the scratch on his forearm. "What was that for?"

"Why do you care? You're dreaming, right?" The cat held out a paw. "Pleased to meet you, by the way. Everyone around here calls me Snowy."

Billy thought about it for a moment, then took the paw in his hand. "My name's Billy…er, Billy Euston." Then, because he couldn't think of anything else to say, he added, "Snowy, an unusual name…especially for a black cat."

Snowy licked his paws. "Daft Aggie named me. I think it's meant to be ironic. Still, it's better than Billy-erbilly any day of the week."

"It's just Billy. Wait a second, Aggie? You mean Aggie Cranbrook? She came to the house earlier, to say hello. Mom says she owns the big mansion at the other end of the village."

In fact, Agatha Cranbrook owned most of the surrounding countryside, including *Adventure Safari* (the nearby zoo and theme park). She'd appeared the previous afternoon with a picnic hamper for them, as a welcome to the village. Billy had been impressed with

19

her, though she did seem a little strange. He hadn't met many old people before. His grandparents had died when he was very young, but even he knew most of them didn't wear jeans, cowboy boots and a T-shirt with the words 'HEAVY METAL ROCKS' printed in giant, red letters across the front. He found himself wondering if Aggie was some kind of modern-day witch.

"Are you Aggie's cat? Did she put a spell on you?"

"A spell? You've been watching too many movies, mate. Aggie's no witch, and I'm certainly not her cat, though I do let her give me food every once in a while. 'Are you her cat?' he says. Bloody cheek."

Billy felt himself blush again. "Sorry."

"Listen, it's late, I should go, but I could really use your help with something. Let's meet up again tomorrow?" He looked at the kitchen clock. "Down by your garden shed, at midday. I'll explain everything. That is, if you haven't woken up by then," he added, with a grin.

Snowy trotted across the tiled floor to the back door. He jumped up to grab the handle. The door swung open. "Any questions?"

"Talking cat, back garden, noon tomorrow. I think I've got it." Billy stood in the doorway, watching Snowy saunter up the garden path, then stared at the clotted blood on his forearm. "And don't mention talking cats to anyone," he added, to himself.

Snowy set off through the woods. Disappointment at the loss of his prized possession tempered by his natural cheery disposition and a huge sense of relief. After all, hadn't he risked everything to get it back? He couldn't have done more. Surely, Missy would have understood. He enjoyed life in Little Chumberry. The villagers gave him food, and since he also enjoyed Razor's protection, the local foxes didn't dare to bother him. Better still, now he'd found a talking human, Razor himself would be forever in his debt. He didn't have to leave after all. For the first time in weeks, he felt safe.

Pleased with his night's work, he began to sing. Unfortunately for any creature unlucky enough to be within earshot, Snowy believed the usual niceties of singing (like keeping in tune, or remembering the words) only applied to other, less sophisticated, vocalists. He made his way through the trees, carrying the tune in the vocal equivalent of a headlock, oblivious to the suffering he caused along the way.

"Don't let the dogs out! No-no-no-no!"

Snowy continued 'singing' until he entered a small clearing, where he froze. Something wasn't right. His ears flattened against the side of his head as he looked about him.

From off to his left came a frantic rustling. Moments later, a muted squeal, cut short by an unpleasant snapping noise. The musty odor of fresh blood wafted toward him. He turned to face the smell.

A fox appeared from behind a small tree, between its jaws, the body of a rat. Snowy didn't move as it crossed the clearing to drop the dead animal at his feet.

It opened its mouth in a cruel smile.

Moonlight glinted off something sharp and pointy.

"Razor, I wish you'd lose the helmet. One of the humans might see you."

The fox shook its head. "I find it useful. Besides,

our dead friend here got quite a surprise when he jumped on me."

Snowy noted the teeth marks on the helmet's leather neck pad. He took in the bloodstained metal spike on top. "So you might say 'He got the point', eh?"

Razor looked unimpressed.

"You know–'got the *point*'? Oh well, please yourself." The would-be assassin wore a metallic collar around its neck, and a surprised expression, now permanently etched, on its dead face.

"It's the fourth this week," Razor said. "No matter where I am, they always find me."

"Never mind that now," Snowy said. "I've found one."

Razor's face lit up. "A talking human?"

"They all talk."

"You know what I mean," Razor snapped.

"His family just moved into the village. We had a nice little chat."

"Did you ask about Fur-Face? Will he help?"

"Don't be daft. The boy just got here. How would he know Fur-Face? I think I can persuade him to help though," Snowy added, when he saw the flash of anger on Razor's face, "but we mustn't rush him." He sat down to rub at his ears with a front paw. "The poor kid thought he was dreaming. Let me work on him a few days, before you meet him."

Razor's eyes glowed in the moonlight. "No, bring him out here tomorrow."

"You're the boss." Snowy looked at the remains of the rat, then cast a nervous glance around the clearing. "Perhaps we should stick together for a while, just in case there are more of 'em about."

"No need. Fur-Face always sends them out alone. I think his voice drives them mad. If he sends more than one, they forget their target and attack each other. You should be safe...tonight."

"Right." Snowy relaxed a little. "Still, we ought to hide the body. Where should we put it?"

Razor sniffed at the carcass. "Leave it to me."

The unsettling gleam in Razor's eye reminded Snowy that under normal circumstances it could easily be his own dead body laying there in the grass. Obviously, the spiky helmet wouldn't be involved, but that did nothing to quell the uneasy sensation which swept over him.

"Of course, right...thanks." He tried to look nonchalant. "I'll let you get on then, shall I? I'll bring the boy out here tomorrow night, when everyone else is asleep. Where shall we find you?"

"Don't worry, cat," Razor said. "I'll find you."

Snowy sidled away. "Good, good, okay. I'll be off then. Bye now." He started off toward the village, trying not to look in too much of a hurry, but when he heard the crunching sound of teeth on bone, instinct took over his paws. He broke into a run.

Chapter Three
'Daft' Aggie

The smell of fried bacon brought Billy downstairs in a hurry. He sat at the breakfast table, half-convinced his encounter with Snowy the previous night had been nothing more than a vivid dream.

Then he remembered the scratch.

He ran his fingertip along the thin scab across his forearm. It really had happened. "Well, at least I'm not crazy," he muttered.

"What was that, dear?" His mother set down a cooked breakfast in front of him.

"Nothing, Mom. I feel much better today."

"I'm glad to hear it, but the next time you decide to come downstairs for a midnight snack, clear up after yourself please." She picked up the glass Snowy had used. "And aren't you a little too old for a bendy straw?"

"Sorry," Billy mumbled, through a mouthful of fried eggs. "Where's Dad?"

"At work. He wasn't supposed to start until Monday, but something urgent came up. I thought we might take Emma for a stroll through the village this morning to visit Aggie, the nice old lady we met yesterday. She invited us over. We can stop off at the village store on the way, to get her a 'Thank you' card for that hamper she gave us."

Why not? Billy thought. I'll be back in plenty of time to meet up with Snowy.

An hour later, the Eustons crunched up the long, gravel driveway to Aggie Cranbrook's Tudor-style mansion. They climbed the stone steps to the front door, where Billy picked up his little sister so she could ring the doorbell.

Once inside, they were ushered into the drawing room by the maid, who looked remarkably familiar.

"Didn't we just see you at the village store?" Mrs. Euston asked.

The maid grinned. "No, dear, I'm *Helen* Roberts. You'll be thinking of my sister, Penny. She owns the store. Mind you, we do look alike, or so we've been told these last forty years or so, which is not surprising really, what with us being identical twins and all. Wait here please. I'll inform Mrs. Cranbrook you've arrived."

She stepped into the hallway, took a deep breath, then bellowed at the top of her voice. "Oi, Aggie! Get a move on will you? You've got visitors!" She paused to straighten a stack of notebooks next to the telephone, then came back into the drawing room to find Billy and his mother staring at her. "Sorry about the shouting. Aggie's fine close up, but the old girl can't hear too well over distance. I think all those rock concerts did her ears in."

Mrs. Euston laughed. "I can just imagine Aggie at a rock concert."

"Oh no, dear. She gave all that up when she went to Africa in the sixties. Mind you, I heard the other band members were none too pleased. They'd just finished a European tour supporting *The Stones*, and it's never easy finding a good drummer, or so I've heard. Anyway, I'm sure she won't be long. Can I get you some tea, Mrs. Euston?" She winked at Emma, who tried to hide behind her mother's leg. "I expect the younglings would like something, too. I'll bring juice, and see if I can't find some interesting biscuits."

While they waited, Billy wandered around the enormous drawing room. Dark, mahogany cupboards lined the walls. Strange, exotic ornaments, marble animals, intricate woodcarvings and dozens of ornate, silver picture frames covered every available flat surface. The smell of furniture polish hung in the air like an invisible cloud.

He picked up an old black-and-white photo. It showed a young man with unusually large lips. He read the inscription: '*To Aggie, The one who got away. All my love, Mick.*' He selected another, more recent, picture of Aggie and a young African man in a safari suit. Both of them wore huge smiles as they stood alongside a baby elephant.

"That's my newest baby. Her name's Alicia."

At the sound of Aggie's Scottish accent, Billy turned to see her smiling at them from the doorway.

"She's only three weeks old, but already weighs 290 pounds." She glanced down at her outfit, a dark blue boiler suit, covered in mud and straw. "Sorry, running a bit behind schedule today. Welcome to my humble home. Let me get changed, then I'll show you around."

Billy found most grownups boring, but Mrs. Cranbrook fascinated him. She somehow made him feel both special and comfortable at the same time. He quite forgot his appointment with Snowy as she took them all on a grand tour of her family home.

All around the house, mementoes and exotic ornaments stood on display. Little Emma kept trying to grab at them.

On the upstairs landing, Billy noticed a crude woodcarving. He couldn't tell if it was meant to represent a horse, or a big dog. It looked out of place alongside the other, more well-crafted, pieces.

"Where did you get this one, Mrs. Cranbrook?"

She picked it up. "You make me sound like a schoolteacher. Do call me 'Aggie', everyone else does. I got this from a young man named Daniel, back when I lived in Kenya during the sixties. He wanted to thank me, so he carved this. He would have been about nine or ten at the time."

She offered the carving to Emma, who went to take it, then changed her mind and buried her face in her mother's shoulder.

"Did you pay for a water well or something?" Mrs. Euston asked.

"Actually, I saved his sister from a leopard, though now you mention it, I think we also sank a well."

Billy's jaw dropped. "You shot a leopard by yourself!"

"Not exactly." Aggie put back the carving and rolled up her sleeve, revealing three deep scar lines on her left forearm. "I only had a spear."

A sad, faraway look came over her face. "It happened as Kiki and I walked back from the river one afternoon. The poor thing was only trying to protect her cubs. She must have seen us as a threat. I tried to shoo her away, but she attacked."

Billy shook his head in wonder. "Aggie, you're amazing."

"Thank you, dear. Now, who fancies a stroll around the garden?"

They stepped outside through a glass door in the main dining room onto the stone patio behind the house. The back yard turned out to be the size of a small park, several hundred yards wide and at least half a mile deep. A long greenhouse stood about fifty yards from the patio. Two men, clad in dark green overalls, knelt at the nearby flowerbeds, digging up weeds. Billy half-expected to see the entrance to a maze somewhere.

Mrs. Euston set Emma down. "What a glorious view."

Billy stared out across the rows of fields at the line of traffic on the main road to the *Adventure Safari* theme park, several miles away. The distant cars looked like insects.

An eight-foot, ivy-covered wall separated the western side of the garden from the main lawn. Aggie ushered them through a green, wooden door on to a narrow path which led them to a gateway, then down some steps and into a cobbled stableyard. Emma took one look at the horses and immediately wanted to ride them.

"When she's older I'll be happy to give her lessons," Aggie said, then took Billy's arm. "Let me show you what we've set up over here."

She led them across the cobbles toward what looked like an oversized, country bungalow.

Inside it seemed more like a zoo.

"Smells like a hospital," Billy said.

They walked down the wide corridor which ran through the middle of the building, looking into each room through wide, glass walls as they passed by.

"We provide medical treatment for the animals from *Adventure Safari*," Aggie said. "We set things up according to their individual needs. We also carry out animal studies. An American company sponsors most of it. They even provide some of the science staff. Those stairs lead down to the research area."

At the end of the corridor, they went through a set of bright red double-doors. Behind it, a staircase and another, even bigger, door, with a digital sign on:

OPERATION IN PROGRESS–DO NOT ENTER!

Aggie put a finger to her lips. "This way, but keep quiet now."

The Eustons followed her up the stairs into a large room. A glass wall surrounded a giant hole in the floor. Aggie gestured to the padded chairs that encircled the observation window. "Have a seat. One of our animals had a bit of an accident last night. They'll be finished in a minute."

Billy looked down into a hospital-style operating theater. Three people, each dressed in blue scrubs and masks, bent over a large, hairy animal. "It's a gorilla."

Emma moved forward to get a closer look. Her hands and face left smudges on the glass when Mrs. Euston picked her up to sit on her lap.

Aggie smiled. "Mr. Tinkles is getting on a bit. He took a bit of a tumble yesterday, damaged his shoulder. He's not as sure-footed as he used to be."

"Oh, the poor thing," Mrs. Euston said. "What can they do?"

"It's the same procedure they'd perform on a human, although, as you can imagine, they had to fully sedate him."

"Will he be okay?" Billy asked.

"Oh yes," Aggie waved to the blue-suited figures as they left the operating room. Two orderlies came in to wheel Mr. Tinkles away. "I've hired one of the best animal surgeons in the country to look after all of my babies. Would you like to meet him?"

The sound of footsteps came up the stairs. Billy turned to greet the chief surgeon, but Emma pushed past him.

"Daddy!" She jumped into her father's arms.

Dr. Euston beamed at his wife. "What a lovely surprise."

"Aggie invited us. She thought you might like a bit of support, for your first operation here."

"I knew you were a vet," Billy said, "but I didn't know you could do gorillas." He thought about his father's many unsuccessful attempts at maintenance work in their old apartment. "Wow."

"And how is your patient?" Aggie asked.

"Doing fine. While he was under, I had a look at that eye infection you mentioned. It's nothing a few drops won't sort out, though getting them in might prove challenging. Still, the operation went well."

After Dr. Euston got cleaned up, they all went to the staff restaurant behind the hospital building. Aggie entertained them with stories about her animal studies in Kenya, then listened with avid interest while Billy told her all about his comic book creation, Static-Man.

Halfway through an explanation about how Static-

Man acquired his amazing super-powers, Billy noticed Snowy on the window ledge outside. The cat looked decidedly grumpy. It pawed at the window, then jerked its head, as a signal for him to come outside.

Aggie turned to see what had caught Billy's attention. "Why it's Snowy. I haven't seen him around for days."

How could I forget to meet up with a talking cat?

Snowy jumped off the window ledge and disappeared from view.

Now where's he going?

A moment later, a tall, bearded man, in a white lab coat, approached their table.

"Hello, Aggie. Hi, Jim," the newcomer said, with a little too much enthusiasm. "So this is why you cancelled our lunch."

Dr. Euston gestured to each of his family in turn. "My wife, Louise, my son, Bill, and the chocolate-covered face there belongs to my daughter, Emma. Everybody, meet Professor Marcus Sedgewick. He runs the research department here."

Billy's mother smiled. "Pleased to meet you, Professor Sedgewick."

The professor beamed at Mrs. Euston.

"Enchanted, Louise, but do please call me Marcus." He bowed low, then kissed the back of her hand.

Billy rolled his eyes. His instant low opinion of the man sank even further when the professor reached over to ruffle his hair. "How's it going, sonny?"

"Fine."

Professor Sedgewick looked at his watch. "Oh well, best get on. You know how it is, lots to do, no time to do it in. Enjoy your tour, everyone." He strode across the crowded cafeteria. As he approached the main door he turned to wave at them and walked straight into a young woman. The unfortunate girl fell backward onto one of the dinner tables. Her food tray flew into the air, scattering its contents in a wide radius.

Billy struggled not to laugh at the sight of a crimson-faced Professor Sedgwick, stammering apologies to the young woman in particular, but also to everyone nearby, who wore varying expressions of anger and amusement, depending on how much of the girl's spaghetti bolognaise had splattered over their clothes and hair.

After accepting the woman's assurances that no lasting harm had been done, the professor apologized one last time, then, quite literally, ran out of the cafeteria.

Mrs. Euston watched him go. "He seems…nice."

Aggie sighed. "Yes, though a little odd. No matter how hard I try, I just can't figure him out."

"I've known Marcus since veterinary college," Dr. Euston said. "He means well and he's great with animals, but people? Not so much."

Billy's mother whisked Emma off to the restroom to wash the chocolate from her face. When they returned, his father went to check on Mr. Tinkles. The others headed back to Aggie's house.

Snowy had vanished.

On their way back through the courtyard they stopped off at the stables. Billy found the smell a little overpowering, so he stood in the doorway, watching Aggie show Emma the best way to stroke a horse.

He heard a voice from by his feet.

"Didn't they teach you to tell the time at school? Or did you just change your mind?"

Snowy sat on the floor beside him, tail twitching.

"*Some* people might think a talking cat is *worth* keeping an appointment with. Oh, and another thing, that sister of yours left a couple of fish-fingers on her plate back there. You just threw 'em away. I'd have had them you know."

"Sorry, I got a bit side-tracked."

"What was that, dear?" Aggie noticed Snowy and smiled. "There's my favorite cat! Come and give your Auntie Aggie a hug." Leaving Mrs. Euston to look after Emma, she scooped up Snowy and cuddled him like a baby.

"Normally, I wouldn't put up with this sort of thing," Snowy said. "At least, not unless there was food on offer, but I'll make an exception in this case, since it gives me an excuse to stay around while we have a chinwag."

Billy looked from Aggie to his mother. *They really can't hear him.*

Snowy lifted his head to let Aggie scratch him under the chin. "From what I can tell, it's got something to do with them brainwave pattern things. Why don't we go back to your place? We can have a proper chat in private, over a nice meal."

"I can't take you home with me."

"Would you like to dear?" Aggie said. "He's not really my cat. Last Christmas, my head gardener found him in a pile of snow by the side of the road. That's why I call him 'Snowy'. The poor wee thing had been hit by a car, so Tom brought him here for help."

Snowy's head jerked forward. "Found me in the road? He was the one who bloody ran me over!"

"One of the vets here had to operate on him right away," Aggie continued, oblivious to Snowy's indignation. "Mind you, I had to threaten him with the sack first. He said he didn't work on 'domestic' animals. To tell you the truth, I've been trying to find him a home. We put up a poster at the scene of the accident, but no one came. Marcus Sedgewick offered to take him last week, but he spends most of his time here. I didn't think it would be fair. I'd keep him myself, only poor Helen's allergic."

Tugging a protesting Emma behind her, Mrs. Euston came closer to inspect Snowy, who did his best to appear loveable. "He looks a bit dirty."

"Dirty? Not me, love. Pure as the driven wet and white stuff me. Tell her, Bill, tell her."

Emma tugged at Snowy's tail. "Emmy want horsy."

"Watch it, girlie. A cat's tail is his castle, or something like that. Anyway, no pulling it, you hear?"

Billy's mother shook her head. "He doesn't look the sort of cat who wants to be owned."

"Owned?" Snowy glared at her. "Who said anything about being owned? I just thought I might, you know, visit for a bit."

Why not? Billy thought. At least he'll be someone to talk to. "Can we keep him?"

His mother looked surprised. "I didn't think you liked animals."

"It might be fun."

"I tell you what," Aggie said. "Why not give it a try

for a week or two? I can always take him off your hands if it doesn't work out."

Billy's mother gave in. "All right, if you're sure it's okay."

"Of course, dear." Aggie gave Snowy a final hug, then handed him to Billy. "But I just know you'll want to keep him. Shall I away and find a travel-box for him?"

Snowy's ears pricked up. "Stuff that for a game of soldiers. Anyone who values the skin on his arms had better not try putting *me* in a box, I can tell you."

"Why don't I just carry him?" Billy said.

Snowy tried to jump down. "I know where you live, you ninny. I'll meet you there."

Billy let go of the struggling cat. "Or maybe he can just follow us home. That way, we'll know he wants to stay with us."

They went on to the house. Snowy trotted along beside them, muttering to himself. Billy couldn't make out much, but he definitely heard the words 'fish-fingers' and 'no consideration' several times.

Aggie waved them off from her front door. "Don't forget, drop in anytime. Emma dear," she added, as the Eustons made their way down the gravel path. "I don't think Snowy wants you to ride him."

Emma had grabbed Snowy's tail. She tried to clamber up on his back. "Giddy-up, horsy."

"Get off me, girl. I'm warning you, my grandfather was a tiger. I'll bite your legs off."

When Billy opened the gate, Snowy darted past him into the wide, country lane followed by Mrs. Euston, who picked up her protesting daughter.

"I think I'll carry her the rest of the way."

They set off through the village. Snowy stayed close, but kept a healthy distance between his tail and little Emma's grasping fingers.

"He does seem to want to be with us," Billy said, when they'd got about halfway home.

Emma had given up trying to get at the cat, and rested her head on her mother's shoulder.

"It certainly looks like it, but isn't *he* supposed to be following *us*?"

"Right, got it, no problem." Ahead of them, Snowy jumped onto a garden wall to let them pass by. "I'll just follow behind at a respectful distance," he added, in a sarcastic voice. "After all, who ever heard of a cat who knew his way around?"

Snowy sulked for the rest of the journey. When they reached the cottage, he hung around in the front yard, refusing to enter, until Billy coaxed him inside by placing a bowl of milk in the hall.

"No straw I notice. How common."

Nevertheless, Snowy drank the milk. A short while later he followed Billy upstairs where he sat on the bed, arguing with his new landlord.

"I could hardly give you a straw in front of my mother could I?" Billy said. "Besides, you managed a second bowl, so it can't have been that unpleasant."

"I needed the extra lot to help me get over the shock. It's not pleasant finding something like that in your food, you know. That great big head, those huge ears, and that evil looking grin." Snowy shuddered. "Ugh, gave me quite a turn it did."

Billy laughed. "It's only a picture. My sister has Mickey Mouse on most of her plates. Anyway, I thought cats liked mice."

"Not when they're smirking at us from the bottom of the bowl we don't. I expect I'll be having nightmares for weeks now. Thank you so very much."

"Exactly what are you?"

Snowy flopped on the bed. "To be honest, I don't really know anymore. One minute I'm washing me ears by the road, the next thing I know, I wake up in a vetstipal, wanting milk served in a glass with a straw in it. Not that anyone would listen," he added, with a sigh.

"What's a 'vetstipal'?"

"You know, where they fix the animals. Anyway, all of a sudden, I understand every word you humans say, though you're the first to notice I can speak your lingo."

"Okay, so you can talk, but why do you want a straw for your milk?"

"I don't know," Snowy stretched out across the duvet. "I keep getting these 'human' urges. I manage to block them out most of the time, though I must admit, I quite like the straw."

Billy sat at his desk, taking notes. "Maybe the collision with the car somehow changed you. I know bumps on the head can affect humans."

"Yeah, cats too. Some tomatoes fell on my brother's head once. The blows affected him all right. They killed him stone dead."

"Don't be silly, a few tomatoes couldn't kill a cat."

"They could if they were still in the can." Snowy sat up and stared out of the window. "Poor old Todger, I told him not to take one from the bottom of the display."

"But how come only I can hear you?" Billy asked,

trying to steer the conversation back into less confusing waters. "Aggie and my mom certainly can't."

Snowy jumped off the bed to claw at the carpet. "I dunno. We went to every house in the village, hoping to make contact with a human, but of all the people we tried, you're the only one who paid any attention."

Billy studied the cat's face. "Your mouth moves a bit when you speak, but it doesn't fit right." He remembered the old kung fu movies he sometimes watched with his father. "It's like you've been badly dubbed."

A question, which had been hovering politely at the back of his mind, now elbowed its way to the front. "*We've* been trying? Don't tell me there are more talking cats out there."

"Not a cat, a fox," Snowy said. "We sort of work together."

"A fox? How did you find him? How come *he* can talk?"

"No idea." Snowy thought for a moment before continuing. "His name's Razor. I never asked him why he can speak human. Until I moved in here, I spent most nights sleeping in the stables behind Daft Aggie's place. The horses don't mind 'cause I scare the rats away, but there's precious little food around, even with the staff restaurant for the research place nearby. They probably take the scraps over to the wildlife park." Snowy jumped onto the desk. "Anyway, I found a good place to eat behind the pub, you know, *The Laughing Milkmaid*. It does leftovers, and I often get 'Rodent Surprise' too, which is a personal favorite."

Billy screwed up his face in disgust. "They cook

rodents?"

"Course not. I mean I sometimes catch mice there, and believe me, they're always surprised. About a month ago, I was hanging about outside the boozer after closing time. I'd just fished a nice bit of chicken from the bin, when I heard a sudden ruckus. I stuck me head out for a look-see, and there was Razor, chasing away this other fox. It gave me quite a turn, I can tell you. I thought for sure I was dog food."

Billy leaned in closer, fascinated. "What happened next?"

"After the other fox scarpered, Razor looked at me kind of funny, then asked how come I could talk human. He said he'd heard me singing their songs. I told him all I knew, then he said I had to find a human to help him. He can't exactly go around looking for one himself, especially with that silly hat he wears. As you can imagine, I didn't argue. He's really keen to meet you. I told him you'd be out in the back garden later, after dark."

Billy surprised himself when he answered. "In that case, I'd better have an early night."

At six-o'clock, to the obvious amazement of his parents, Billy volunteered to go to bed early. He pushed away his empty dinner plate, leaned back, stretched out his arms and let out a theatrical yawn. "I feel *so* tired . It must be all this country air. I think I'll head upstairs to bed."

"Dear oh dear," Snowy muttered, from under the table. "What a ham."

Emma giggled, then dropped another one of her fries on the floor for him.

* * *

A short while later, Emma sat on the upstairs landing, playing with her Pretty Pony doll as she listened to the whispered argument going on behind the closed bathroom door.

"What do you think you're doing? Get down off Emma's potty."

Someone flushed the toilet.

Another voice, this one brimming with indignation. "I only stood on it so I could reach, and I lifted the seat up, didn't I?"

"You're supposed to go in the litter box my dad brought home for you, or outside in the garden."

"Oh that's charming that is. How come you get to use a proper loo, and I have to wee in a miniature sandpit? Just 'cause I'm a cat doesn't mean I don't have rights. I *am* a guest here you know."

"Well, all right, but just make sure you don't do anything like this in front of the others."

Emma heard the sound of running water, followed by the hum of an electric toothbrush.

"And put that down. That's my dad's."

She laughed. "Silly horsy."

To the two-year-old, a talking cat seemed no more unusual than a seven-foot singing bear, a comic 'wabbit', or the endless line of cute, chatty creatures which talked to her from the television set each day. She picked up the Pretty Pony toy and toddled off to her room.

Chapter Four
A Midnight Meeting

In his dream, Billy was Static-Man's trusty sidekick, Electric Bill. Together they'd just foiled The Dark Shadow's latest plot. Church bells rang in celebration while delighted crowds chanted his name, though now he came to think of it, it was more of a whisper than a cheer.

"Bill… Bill… Wake up. Time to go."

He opened his eyes to see a furry face staring back at him, so close, their noses touched. Snowy jumped off his chest as he sat up.

Billy waved a hand in front of his face. "Phew! I think you overdid it with my dad's mouthwash."

"Think yourself lucky, it's usually Essence of Leftovers. Get a move on, Razor doesn't like to be kept waiting."

Billy became aware of a muffled ringing from under the bedclothes, down by his feet. Still half-asleep, he groped around at the bottom of the bed to switch off his alarm clock. "Why can't your friend keep more sociable hours?"

"He's a fox. To him, this is sociable hours."

Billy got dressed. Then, with Snowy following close behind, he crept downstairs.

Moonlight flooded the kitchen. He moved the box

of soap powder from in front of the hole in the back door his father had cut out earlier. It was supposed to be for a cat flap, but he'd made it several inches too wide.

Snowy darted through, then stuck his head back inside. "Don't bother unlocking the door, just follow me through here."

"It's not *that* big."

After dinner, Dr. Euston had spent much of the evening in the back yard, clearing out the flower beds and chopping back overgrown tree branches. He'd disposed of the cuttings by burning them in an old metal bin. The acrid smell of smoke still hung in the air as they made their way to the shed.

"I still can't believe I let you talk me into this."

Snowy jumped on the roof, where he settled down to lick at his paws. "Kids today have no sense of adventure."

"And you never did tell me what you were looking for in my room."

Snowy stopped licking. "It doesn't matter now. It got chucked away."

"Sorry," Billy said. "Maybe I can get you a new one. What was it?"

"Just an old squeaky toy. It belonged to my sister."

"I didn't know you had a sister."

"Oh yes. I was one of five. There was me, though back then my name was Roland, then Todger, Bernard, Reg and Missy."

"Where are they now? Do you ever see them?"

Snowy stretched out on the black roofing felt. "Let me think. I told you about Todger, didn't I? Bernard does TV commercials. Reg went to live on a dairy farm, and Missy went with me to live with a family in town. Poor Reg died last summer. He drowned in a vat of double-whipped cream. I heard he kept afloat for nearly an hour before he finally went under."

"How awful!"

"Well, he would have gone sooner, but he climbed out a couple of times to use the toilet."

"You're joking."

"Of course, at least about my brothers anyway. How do I know what happened to 'em? Cats don't get to keep in touch with their family like humans do. Don't remember much. One minute we're all messing around, having a play-fight, the next thing I know, me and Missy are looking at the back seat of a motor through a hole in a cardboard box."

Billy leaned back against the shed door. "What happened then?"

"This young couple took us to live with them. Missy took it hard. She really missed Mom and the others, but I looked out for her, and they treated us well. We stayed with them for three years. Then the woman had a baby. We didn't think anything of it at first, but soon after, a man turned up at their house with a big cat box. They gave him some money and he took us away. It makes sense really," Snowy added. "I mean, why would humans want a couple of cats around when they've got their own baby?"

"They should have thought about that before they took you in."

"Anyway, we just figured we'd be going to live with this new bloke. He put us in his car and drove out of town. When Missy saw all the fields and stuff, she figured he must live on a farm or something. She kept saying it would be fun 'cause we'd have more room, but when he parked on a high bridge over the river, I knew something wasn't right."

Billy noticed the tremble in Snowy's voice as he went on.

"He did Missy first. She actually went to him. She never could see the bad in humans. He grabbed her by the scruff of the neck, then flung her over the side of the bridge. She was too surprised to make a sound, but I'll never forget the look on her face as she started to drop."

Snowy clawed at the shed roof. "I scratched him good when he came for me. In the end he held the cat box out over the water. I expected him to drop it, with me still inside, but he just held it upside-down and started shaking it. I suppose he didn't want to have to buy a new one. I remember the cage door flapping about. I could see the water, thirty feet below me. I tried to hang on, but my paws kept slipping. In the end I decided, stuff it, and I let go."

Billy's throat went dry. He stepped away from the shed, where he could look at Snowy "No wonder you don't like cat boxes."

Snowy jumped off the roof and onto the water barrel. "I haven't thought about that night for a long time."

"How did you survive?"

"Dunno. I woke up on the riverbank sometime the next day. I searched everywhere for Missy, but I never found her. When I realized she hadn't made it, I got angry. I decided, no matter how long it took, somehow, I'd find that git of a human and rip his bloody throat out." Snowy sighed. "But before I even got back into town, Aggie's idiot gardener hit me with his car."

"Maybe Missy did make it," Billy said. "Maybe she came ashore somewhere downriver. She could be out there right now, trying to find you."

Snowy sniffed at some dried leaves on the lid of the barrel. "No. After Aggie had me fixed up, I spent weeks searching, but all I found of her was that rubber toy. She had it in the cat box with her when the man took us. Missy's gone. She was my only real friend. Now I'm alone. I've learned to accept it."

After a long silence, Billy reached over to stroke Snowy's head. "You don't have to be alone anymore. I'll be your friend. If you like."

A cold, hard voice cut through the moment. "How touching, how very…human."

Billy turned to see a fox sitting on the grass, just a few feet away. It wore a spiky, metal helmet on its head. The animal's cold stare unnerved him. "Hello, you must be Razor."

"How perceptive of you." Razor's voice dripped with sarcasm. "I expect my ability to talk gave me away."

"Actually the silly hat did," Billy snapped, stung by the fox's condescending manner.

"He-he, nice one, Bill," Snowy said. "Now come on, Razor, don't be rude. Bill's a good kid. You can trust him, I do."

"Foxes avoid other animals," Razor said, "especially humans. I find this very unnatural, but I will try to trust you."

"Then I'll try to be worthy of it. Seriously though,

why *do* you wear the helmet?"

"It tells me when the others are near."

"Others? I thought only you and Snowy could talk."

"Fur-Face can make lesser animals understand and carry out basic instructions."

"How does the helmet help? Can you hear their thoughts or something?"

"Not thoughts exactly," Razor said. "When his rats are near, I feel their anger, their fear, their hate."

"So what about Snowy? Do you feel anything when he's around?"

Razor looked at Snowy, who had clambered back onto the shed roof. "You mean, apart from an overwhelming desire to stop him singing?"

"Oi! Watch it you."

Billy grinned. "You're not as mean as you make out." He gestured at the helmet. "Mind if I take a closer look?"

"I shall try to control my instinct to bite, but don't make any sudden moves."

Billy got down on his knees to examine the helmet. On closer inspection, the spike turned out to be a radio aerial, though the top had been snapped off, leaving a sharp, jagged edge.

"This looks like some kind of reception device. Who gave you this?"

Razor bared his teeth. "Fur-Face. He believed it would control me. He was wrong."

Still on his knees, Bill sat back. "Who's this Fur-Face you keep talking about?"

"A human," Snowy said. "Razor says he works at the vetstipal."

Billy shifted into a more comfortable sitting position, with his back against the shed door. "If I'm to help, you must tell me everything."

Razor looked skyward. "It started about a moon-cycle ago. Many humans came crashing through the woods in the middle of the day. We thought they'd come to drive us out for the hunt. My mate, Scala, stayed in the lair with our two cubs while I tried to lead the men away, but they went straight to our foxhole. Two of them blocked the back exits. Another set up a machine in front of the entrance. Smoke came out of a tube, which he pushed into our home, while a fourth human stood ready with a big net."

Razor fell silent.

"Sorry," Billy said. "This must be hard for you."

"I heard the cubs whimpering, and Scala trying to calm them down. I had to do something, so I threw myself at the machine, hoping to push it over, but one of the humans hit me with a shovel. I woke up in a big white room. Someone had shaved the fur from my head. It felt cold and it hurt." Razor pulled back his lips in a fierce snarl. "Then I saw Fur-Face. He stood outside my cage, staring at me through the bars."

"What happened then?"

"I found I could understand him. Fur-Face gave instructions to another human, somewhere behind him. He said something about 'reception levels'. The other human came over with a metal box. It breathed on my face. It made me drowsy. I fell over."

"He probably used MASC on you," Billy said. "It stands for 'Mobile Anesthetic Spray Canister'. It's used to sedate dangerous animals. My dad mentioned it at dinner. He says he'll need to spray Mister Tinkles so he can get close enough to put his eye drops in."

The two animals stared at him.

"Sorry, I thought you'd want to know."

"Go on, Razor." Snowy looked at Billy over invisible glasses. "We're listening."

Razor scratched at his nose. "Fur-Face opened my cage. I tried to get away, but my legs wouldn't work. I couldn't even stand. His assistant carried me to the bench, then held my head while Fur-Face put this on me." He touched the metal helmet with a paw. It gave a tiny 'plink'.

"Fur-Face gave me orders like 'sit' and 'come here', but I ignored him. He grew angry with me."

Billy leaned forward, fascinated. "How did you escape?"

"The human assistant, I think Fur-Face called him 'Gallstone', said the reception might be better in the open air. They put me in a dark box and took me outside. I felt stronger by then, but lay still, feigning weakness. When they opened the box, darkness had fallen. We were on the edge of the wood. Fur-Face moved a few feet away. He ordered me to come to him. Gallstone stood ready with a blanket, in case I tried to escape. I pretended to obey and staggered out onto the grass. Fur-Face got really excited. He started dancing and clapping. Then I ran."

"Good for you," Billy said, "but didn't they come after you?"

Razor's head drooped.

"Fur-Face nearly caught me straight away. He grabbed the top of my helmet, but it snapped off.

Gallstone threw the blanket, but I dodged it and ran off through the woods, back to my family. I had to find out if they escaped."

"Were they all right?" Billy had a horrible feeling he already knew the answer.

"The lair was empty. If he hasn't killed them, Fur-Face has them at the vetstipal compound. I told you he can control some animals. Every night he sends one of his rats after me, but the helmet warns me when they get close." Razor stopped pacing. "I can't get into the compound. I need a human to search in there for my family. Snowy says I can trust you, will you help?"

Billy thought for a moment. "Why would this man, Fur-Face, do all this? I can't see what anyone would have to gain by controlling a fox."

On the shed roof, Snowy stopped licking the inside of his hind leg and sat up. "I know. If he can make foxes obey him, he could order them to stay away from all the farmers' chickens and stuff. I bet they'd pay good money not to have to keep putting up all those wire fences."

Razor shook his head in disgust. "Unbelievable. Did you work that out all by yourself?"

Snowy grinned, blissfully unaware of Razor's sarcasm.

"Yes, maybe," Billy said, not wanting to hurt the cat's feelings, "but I wonder if he might also have something bigger in mind."

"Ooh, I know," Snowy said, keen to improve on his first brilliant deduction. "Now try to stay with me here. Maybe Fur-Face is planning..." he paused for dramatic effect, "...blackmail." He tapped his nose with a front paw. "I bet he means to tell those farmers to pay him loads of money, or else he'll order the foxes to go and kill their chickens. I reckon they'd pay plenty to save all those eggs."

He looked pleased with himself, until Razor let out a low growl.

"Will you stop twittering on about chickens, you halfwit!"

"Well, pardon me for talking. At least I *had* an idea. I don't hear you coming up with any suggestions. I suppose you know all about Fur-Face's plans, Mr. 'I've got a tin can on me 'ead so I know more than everyone else.' Go on then, Chrome-top, what do you think he's up to?"

"I don't know his plans," Razor snarled, "but I guarantee they don't include chickens, you brainless waste of a cat skin."

"Shut your face, Tin-head."

"Why don't you just come down here and make me, Fur-ball."

"Go stick your head in a bucket," Snowy hissed. "Oh wait, I see you already did."

Razor snarled, then crouched, ready to spring.

Things might have got unpleasant then, if Billy hadn't jumped to his feet and moved in between them. "Stop it, the pair of you. You're acting like a couple of kids." The stress of moving home and the strange events of the past couple of days had taken their toll. Something inside him snapped. He shook an angry finger at Razor. "Now listen to me. I'm thirteen years old, which means I have enough problems already, without worrying about talking animals and lost families. If you two keep bickering, I'm going back to bed right now, and you can damn well find someone else to help you. Is that clear?"

Billy glared at the fox. As the first flush of anger receded, a little voice in his head questioned the wisdom of shaking a finger under the nose of a wild animal, especially one with sharp teeth. He folded his arms.

"Yeah, you tell him," Snowy said, from the shed roof. He smirked at Razor over Billy's shoulder.

"And you can stop winding him up. Now, apologize to each other, or I go back inside. I mean it."

The three of them waited in angry silence. Razor spoke first. "Your human friend's got a bit of a temper on him."

"That's nothing, mate," Snowy said. "You should hear him when you leave the cap off the toothpaste. Humans, huh, what can you do?"

Razor pawed at the grass. "Sorry I got angry," he mumbled.

"S'all right," Snowy muttered. "Me too."

Billy took charge while things were calm. "Well done. Now, we need to figure out how to find Razor's family."

"We need a plan," Snowy said, "or better yet, a miracle."

"That would help, but I think we also need Aggie."

Snowy's head jerked up. "Daft Aggie, what can she do?"

"Think about it," Billy said. "The research center's on her land. So's the animal hospital."

The two animals exchanged confused glances.

"All right, the 'vetstipal' then, but she must know what kind of research they do there."

Razor let out a derisive snort. "If this human owns the land, then she's involved."

"No way," Snowy said. "Aggie's one of the good guys!"

Billy remembered the anxious look on Aggie's face while his father had operated on Mr. Tinkles. "I agree. She loves animals. She can't possibly know."

"Having said all that, Bill," Snowy said. "They don't call her Daft Aggie for nothing. The old dear's been good to me. I like her a lot, but even if she wanted to help, what can she do?"

"I don't know, but I can't manage this alone. We need help, so unless you can think of a better idea, I'm going to see her tomorrow."

Snowy raised a paw. "Just a thought, what exactly do you plan to say? The minute you mention me and old Tin-head, Aggie'll think you've gone off your rocker."

"I'll think of something, but right now I need to get some sleep." Billy crouched in front of Razor. "Don't worry, if Fur-Face still has them in the compound, I'll find them for you, I promise."

"Let me know how you get on." Razor scrambled over the garden fence and disappeared into the woods.

Halfway up the path on the way back to the house, Billy realized Snowy hadn't followed him. He turned back to see the cat walking across the next-door neighbor's back yard. "Aren't you coming?"

"You go on without me. Today's Friday. That means Karaoke night down at the pub. There'll be some tasty, roast chicken leftovers waiting for me in the bins down there."

Billy's jaw dropped. "But you ate a whole tin of cat

food at tea time, how can you possibly be hungry?"

"I'm a cat. We're always hungry. See you later." Snowy squeezed through a gap in the fence and trotted off in the direction of *The Laughing Milkmaid*.

The luminous green display on the kitchen microwave read 1:35. Billy poured himself a glass of milk from the fridge, then sat at the kitchen table, already regretting his rash promise to help Razor. "I have no idea what to do," he muttered. "I don't know anyone here. I don't even know my way around. How on earth am I going to find a vixen and two cubs?"

He rinsed out the glass, leaving it upside-down on the tea towel by the sink. After two nights of broken sleep, his body demanded rest. He climbed the stairs, feeling more exhausted with each step, then tiptoed down the hall to his bedroom, wondering whether he should even bother getting undressed for bed. Without making a sound, he opened the door and went inside.

As he closed it behind him, someone turned on his bedside lamp.

"Where the bloody hell have you been?"

Chapter Five
Carmen, Kippers, and Clues

Billy let go of the door handle and turned around.

His father sat on the edge of the bed, arms folded across his chest and an expression of worried anger on his face. "I asked you a question, son. Where have you been?"

"I… I…" Billy struggled to come up with an appropriate answer. "I…needed the toilet?"

"Don't be a smart-aleck." His father jumped up and jabbed an angry finger at him. "Since when do you wear day-clothes to use the bathroom in the middle of the night? Tell me what you were doing outside. The truth this time."

The truth, Billy thought. You can't handle the truth. Suddenly, his exhausted brain produced a decent answer. Out loud he said, "I had a bad dream. I couldn't get back to sleep. I decided a bit of fresh air would help me settle down."

"Rubbish. Who did you meet in the back garden?"

He opened his mouth to answer, but his father interrupted. "I saw you." He gestured to the bedroom window. "Out there, talking to someone down by the shed."

"That was Snowy, Dad."

"Talking to Snowy?" Dr. Euston looked bewildered

for a moment, then the color drained from his face. "Oh God. It's drugs isn't it? You got yourself on some kind of hallucinogenic drugs."

"What? No. Of course not. I meant Snowy was in the garden too. He followed me outside, but wouldn't come back with me. I was trying to coax him in. Honest, Dad, I'd never do drugs."

His father didn't answer straight away. He flopped down in the dark blue swivel chair by the desk. Billy stared at him, unsure what to do.

Finally, he spoke. "Promise me. On Emma's life, promise me you don't do drugs."

"I don't, and I never will."

"All right. But no more nighttime excursions, is that clear?"

"Crystal."

"That's my boy, now back into bed. I'll see you tomorrow."

When Billy eventually came downstairs the next morning, his mother looked pointedly at the kitchen clock.

"This country air has tired everyone out. Emma's still fast asleep. I hope you get used to it before you start your new school; which reminds me, we need to go into town to organize your uniform."

"Oh, mom, the summer break just started. I don't want to think about school or homework for at least another six weeks." Billy glanced around the kitchen. His gaze settled on the oversized hole in the back door. "Have you seen Snowy?"

His mother set a plate of scrambled eggs in front of

him. "That cat of yours is a bottomless pit. He came in from the garden when I did my toast, making pitiful, whining noises and rubbing his tummy until I gave him some cat food. I didn't realize your father already fed him, until I put the empty can in the recycle bin."

Billy reached for the ketchup. "He's a cat, they're always hungry."

His mother poured them both a cup of tea, then sat across the kitchen table from him. She leaned back in her chair and took a sip, all the while, studying his face. "You look happy. Are you beginning to like it here? Your dad and I got a little worried when you started hearing voices the other night."

Billy thought for a while before answering. Clearly his father hadn't discussed the previous night's confrontation with her. "It's not as bad as I expected." He remembered his promise to Razor. "Could I visit Aggie again?"

"Why?"

He gave an innocent smile. "Well, she's a lot of fun, and she did say to visit whenever we liked. Besides," he added, deciding to appeal directly to his mother's maternal instincts. "I bet Aggie knows all the children in the village. She can tell me which ones are well-behaved enough for me to be friends with."

His mother laughed. "All right, you win. No need to lay it on so thick. I'll call Aggie, and if she say's it's okay, you can go this afternoon, but not by yourself."

Billy started to argue that he was old enough to go out alone, when he had a better idea. "Okay, I'm sure Emma would love to see the horses again."

That way, he thought, I can get some time alone

with Aggie while you take Emma to the stables. "I'll bring Snowy too. She likes him."

Mrs. Euston went into the living room to make the arrangements, leaving Billy to finish his breakfast.

"You're a crafty one," Snowy said, as he stepped in through the hole in the back door.

"You heard all that did you?" Billy whispered. "With any luck, we'll have some answers for Razor by this afternoon."

"Maybe. So what's the plan? We sneak in, nose about in Aggie's private papers and solve the case?"

"Not exactly, but I hope we can find out something."

"That'll please old Tin-head."

Billy took a bite of his toast. "You don't like him much do you?"

"What's to like? He's an arrogant so and so, though I suppose you don't need friends when you're top of your own food chain."

"So why help him? You could easily move away from here. He'd never find you."

"I'm not so sure." Snowy scratched at the doormat. "Besides, how many other animals around here can talk human? Plus, he's lost his family, and I know how that feels. If I can help Razor find Scala and their cubs, I will."

"You're just an old softy really, aren't you?"

"Yeah, yeah, all heart me." Snowy jumped onto an empty chair. "You gonna eat all your scrambled egg?"

Later that afternoon, they went to Aggie's mansion. A pretty young girl opened the front door. She had long, black hair, dark brown eyes, and a confident smile. Billy thought she looked about his age.

"Hi, I'm Carmen. You must be the Eustons. Come on in." She frowned at Snowy. "Hello, trouble. I had to go to the village store this morning, thanks to you."

"What did he do?" Billy asked.

Carmen held the door open for them. "He came here last night, after Aggie brought me home from the station. He kept sniffing at my bottle of cola. I thought he wanted to try some, but after he knocked it over and made a mess all over the kitchen table, he wouldn't go near it."

"Of course not," Snowy said. "If I don't drink from the bottle I get sticky whiskers."

"No Helen today?" Mrs. Euston asked.

"Helen runs the village store for her sister on weekends. That's when Penny cooks the meals at *The Laughing Milkmaid*. It gets very busy there, because of all the visitors from the theme park."

Aggie stood up from the sofa as they entered the lounge. Billy smiled when he saw the picture on her T-shirt, a cartoon drawing of a sweet old lady in a wheelchair, waving an umbrella in the air. The words '**Stuff the bingo. Bring me a beer!**' were printed in big red letters underneath. "I see you've met my lovely granddaughter. Isn't she pretty? Looks more like her mother every time I see her." She winked at Carmen. "Although I'm glad to say, she gets her rebellious spirit from my side of the family."

"Oh, Grandma," Carmen's face turned crimson. She looked at Billy and they exchanged the 'What can you do?' glance, shared by children throughout the ages, whenever older relatives embarrassed them in front of each other.

"She's smart too. Do you like the T-shirt she made me, Bill?"

"Very nice."

Snowy jumped onto the arm of the sofa. He rolled over on his back, trying to look pitiful. "Come on, woman, take the hint. I haven't eaten since lunchtime. That was half an hour ago, I'm starving." He looked at Billy, who stared back at him in disbelief. "Well I am."

"Ah, my favorite cat." Aggie picked him up, cradling him in her arms like a baby. "I bet you'd like a drop of milk and something to eat. We had kippers earlier, I'm sure we had some left over."

Mrs. Euston sat on the sofa, with Emma on her lap. "Honestly, Aggie, he just ate, and he had two tins of cat food this morning. I don't want him to get any fatter than he already is."

Snowy glowered at her. "Mind your own beeswax, lady. This is kippers we're talking about."

"You're right of course." Aggie prodded Snowy's more than ample belly. "Who's got a little podgy tum-tum-tummy?" She set him down on the leather sofa. "Just some milk then. Carmen, dear, why don't you take Billy into the kitchen to sort out some drinks?"

Snowy stomped past Mrs. Euston toward the door. "Thank you very much, I don't think. And I'm not fat, just big-boned."

Billy hadn't seen the kitchen on his previous tour. "I thought we had a big kitchen, but this is enormous."

Carmen poured out a saucer of milk and set it on the floor. "Aggie says you just moved here."

"Yes, on Thursday." Billy tried to ignore Snowy's complaints about the lack of a straw. "Though it seems a long time ago. Do you live here with Aggie?"

Carmen took a carton of pineapple juice from the fridge. "Only during the holidays. I got here last night. My parents divorced when I was six. Most of the time I live in Paris with my mother, but I stay here during the summer. Mom organizes some kind of fashion show in August. It gets very busy over there. She thinks I'll get into trouble on my own. She's probably right." Carmen pointed to a tray by the sink. "Hand me that, would you? Still, I don't mind. Aggie's a lot of fun."

Billy felt disappointed. He hadn't seen any children his own age around the village, and rather hoped Carmen would turn out to be a local.

"What about your father, do you see him often?"

"No!" She smiled. "Sorry, I haven't seen him since they split up. Not that I saw much of him before then," she added, with a hint of bitterness.

"That must have been hard."

"Well, *c'est la vie*." She lowered her voice. "I'm not supposed to know about this. Aggie's his mother, but she disowned him. My dad got sent to prison. I don't know what for. He's out now, though. He sometimes writes to my mom, but she won't write back. One time, I sneaked a look at a letter he sent her. He wanted money. Do you know he didn't even ask about me? So I decided, if he doesn't care about his only daughter, then I don't care about him."

Billy didn't know what to say. A few friends back at his old school had just the one parent. He tried to imagine what it would be like without having his dad around for a play-fight or to share a silly joke with, or not being able to confide in his mother when he had something on his mind.

A gurgled belch interrupted the silence.

"Pardon me," Snowy said. "Still, better out than in."

Carmen laughed. "Come on. I'll take the tray, you get the door. I'm glad you've moved here," she added. "It'll be nice to have a new friend for the summer."

Aggie suggested they took their drinks into the garden. They all went outside, except for Snowy, who curled up on the sofa, pretending to be asleep.

"Don't worry about him," Billy said. "He's still sulking about those kippers."

"It wouldn't surprise me one bit," Aggie said. "Sometimes I think that cat understands every word I say."

They stepped into the warm sunshine.

Billy sat on the wide swing-chair on the stone patio with Carmen, while his mother and Emma wandered down the western side of the garden for a tour of the flowerbeds with Aggie. "Did you really make Aggie's T-shirt?"

"Of course." Carmen brushed her hair out of her eyes. "I designed it on the computer, then printed it on some special paper. After that, all I had to do is iron it on. You have to remember to print it back to front though," she added, "or else it comes out funny. I'll show you how to do it sometime, if you want."

"Thanks," Billy said. "I only ever play games on my PC, though I wish I had some software to help me with the comic book I made up. I have to draw everything by hand, which sucks, 'cause I'm not very good."

He looked at Carmen, half expecting her to laugh, but she didn't.

"Then we have something in common."

"You draw comic books?"

"Not exactly. I mean, you're a designer like me. Except I do clothes while you do stories."

"I never looked at it like that. The kids at my old school thought it was a bit childish, except for Patrick."

Carmen took a long sip of juice. "If it makes you happy and doesn't harm anyone, then give it all you've got. That's what Aggie always says. Who's Patrick?"

"My best friend."

They chatted away. She told him about life in France, then he told her all about London and the world he'd left behind. Time flew by, until an hour later when Emma ran up to present them with a big fat worm. Aggie and Mrs. Euston came up behind her, laughing.

"You two have plenty to talk about," Aggie said. She held out her hands to pull Billy and Carmen up from the swing-chair. "How about some ice cream from the cafeteria? We can stop off to see the horses on the way."

"Can I just check on Snowy first?" Billy said. "I'll only be a minute."

He hurried back into the house, but Snowy had disappeared. After checking the kitchen he headed back through the drawing room on his way out to the garden, but someone called to him from the upstairs landing.

"Pssst, up here." With furtive steps, Snowy came down the polished wooden staircase.

"Don't tell me you've been looking for Aggie's office. I didn't want you to go sneaking around. I told you, I'll ask her outright, when I get the chance. Did you find out anything?"

"Well," Snowy lowered his voice. "I had a good sniff around. No mention of foxes in the papers Aggie keeps in her wall safe." He glanced back upstairs. "So I used the laptop in her bedroom to hack into the main computer at the research center. Nothing there either, though I could see there've been a lot of files deleted in the last couple of weeks. I'd say somebody's trying to cover their tracks."

Billy's stared at him, dumbfounded. "Incredible! You found out all that by yourself?"

"Of course not, you great twit. I've been having a nap. How would I know how to work a computer? I'm a cat. The only hacking I do, is when I need to get rid of a fur-ball. Even if I could it wouldn't help," he added. "I can only read numbers."

"Oh, sorry. Wait a minute, then why were you sneaking around upstairs?"

Now Snowy looked embarrassed. "I needed the toilet. I couldn't open the door to the loo down here, so I used the one on the landing. By the way," he added, "I'd leave it a while if you were planning to go, the air up there's a bit chewy at the moment."

"Ew!"

Snowy clambered back on the sofa. "What am I supposed to do? Open a window? Besides, it's your fault for giving me that scrambled egg this morning."

"Forget it," Billy said. "Aggie's taking us for ice cream at the cafeteria by the hospital," he corrected himself, "vetstipal. Coming?"

"Nah, they won't let me in there, but I might pop down later, to scout around for a bit. See if I can find some clues."

"Yeah, right. You mean scraps."

Billy caught up with the others at the stables. Emma wore a huge smile beneath a bright yellow hard hat as she sat proudly astride a Shetland pony. His mother and Carmen stood on either side of her, holding her in place while Aggie took a picture. The pony ignored everyone and munched hay from the ground.

Afterward, they went to the cafeteria and ate ice cream at the same table they'd sat at the day before. Oh well, Billy thought, it's now or never I suppose. He took a deep breath. "Aggie, what sort of research goes on here?"

Aggie dabbed at the side of her mouth with a paper towel. "I'm afraid I can't tell you. Although the truth is, I don't know much about it myself. They pay a lot of money to help me keep the theme park going, and occasionally help me obtain some rare species from abroad." She took a sip of her cola. "You'd be surprised how much red tape one has to get through, to keep something like *Adventure Safari* going. In return, I let them use the research center and work with some of the animals."

"Has it got anything to do with animal communication?" Billy asked.

"Goodness me," his mother said. "What a peculiar question." She took Emma's hand. "I think someone needs to wash her face." She dragged her protesting daughter to the toilets for a clean-up.

"I just wondered."

"Maybe they want to make animal soldiers,"

Carmen said. "I saw a film once, where they taught monkeys to fly bombers."

"Oh no," Aggie frowned. "There'll be none of that kind of thing happening while I'm around. Any breakthrough in animal communication is only for use in promoting mutual understanding and cooperation between species. I insisted they put a clause to that effect in the contract." She clapped a hand over her mouth. "Oh dear. Well, since you'd guessed already, they can't say I told you any secrets."

"I wonder how they do it," Carmen said. "It can't be hand signals, they've been experimenting with those for years. Maybe they insert microchips in their brains."

Aggie folded her arms indignantly. "They better not insert microchips in *my* animals."

"It was just an idea," Carmen said. She turned to Billy, who stared at his ice cream cone, lost in thought. "How do *you* think they do it?"

Billy didn't answer. He kept thinking about Razor. He'd meant to ask him about it the previous night, but then Snowy had started on about chickens, and the question had been driven from his mind. "Why would they shave his head?"

"Shave whose head?" Carmen asked.

Billy looked up. "Sorry, miles away. What did you say?"

Across the table, Aggie groaned. "Oh no, not him again."

Following her gaze, Billy watched Professor Sedgewick stride across the cafeteria to join them. "Hello again. Bill, right? So I guess these empty chairs belong to Little Miss Chocolate-Chops and your lovely mother. But I don't know this young lady?" Marcus stared at Carmen. "Now, Aggie, I never knew you had a younger sister."

Carmen laughed, even Billy smiled.

"Marcus, meet my granddaughter, Carmen. She's staying with me for the school holidays. Carmen, this is Professor Marcus Sedgewick."

"Delighted to meet you, Professor. I'm curious, are you saying I look old, or Aggie looks young?"

Sedgewick's smile faded. "Oh no, I didn't mean... That is, I was trying to..." He looked flustered, then his eyes fixed on something outside the window. "What's old Snowy doing behind that tree?"

Everyone turned to look at Snowy, who stood on his hind legs with his back pressed against a tree trunk, his front paws by his sides. As they watched, he craned his neck to peek at something, then dashed across the path before disappearing out of sight behind a hedge.

"That is one strange cat," Aggie said.

Marcus grinned. "I remember when Tom brought him in last winter. He'd have died if you hadn't ordered old Farofas to fix him up."

A fierce look came over Aggie's face "Nasty little man. He didn't want to help. He even had the cheek to tell me he had no anesthetic available, when I could see that horrid assistant of his, trying to stand in the way so I wouldn't notice the bottle of enhanced Propofol, right there on the workbench. It made me quite cross, I can tell you."

"What did you do?" Carmen asked.

Aggie took another sip of cola. "I knew I couldn't trust them, so I stood there and watched while they

66

operated on poor Snowy. I told Doctor Farofas, 'If that cat dies, you'll have me to deal with.' Luckily for them, Snowy survived, but their attitude made me so cross, I had them both removed. The Americans didn't want them to go, but I insisted."

"Serves them right," Carmen said, "but what about the communication studies? Didn't him leaving cause problems."

Marcus looked surprised.

"It's all right," Aggie said. "They know about the research."

Marcus sat in one of the empty chairs and stroked his beard. "Doctor Farofas didn't have anything to do with the main project. His research focused on active brain responses. Apparently, animals have huge parts of their brains which they almost never access, just like humans. Oh dear." He stood up to wipe at the melted chocolate on the seat of his trousers. "I take it young Emma sat here."

Carmen leaned forward, intrigued. "How would unused brains help people to communicate with animals?"

Marcus sat on the edge of Emma's seat. "Farofas believed all animals, including humans, have a common brain function. He theorized that by finding a way to awaken that function, he could communicate with it."

"Ridiculous," Aggie snorted. "Animals don't have the necessary facial equipment to talk."

"Perhaps they wouldn't have to," Billy said. "Maybe it was something more basic, like telepathy."

Marcus nodded. "Smart boy. Farofas believed he could tap into the animal's brain through its primal emotions and direct it. He certainly had some success with rats. One of his reports says he could make them attack each other."

Carmen shuddered. "How awful."

"What happened to him?" Billy asked.

Marcus stood as Billy's mother returned with Emma. "Like Aggie said, he left. I haven't seen either of them since February, when Gladstone came back to collect all their stuff."

"Gladstone?" Billy felt a rush of excitement. "Was he Doctor Farofas's assistant?"

Aggie pushed back her chair. "Yes, and good riddance to the pair of them. Come along everyone, let's get back to the house and see if we can't find those kippers for Snowy, maybe he can have them for his tea. Goodbye, Professor, see you tomorrow at the Summer Fayre. Are you quite prepared?"

"Absolutely." Marcus beamed. "I've been rehearsing with the rest of the lads for weeks."

As they walked back through the stableyard, Billy strolled along behind the others. He hadn't found out anything about Razor's family, but he felt certain that, whatever was going on, Aggie had nothing to do with it. He also felt pretty sure he'd discovered the identity of the mysterious 'Fur-Face'.

Another question popped into his mind. "Aggie, what's Marcus going to be doing at the Summer Fayre?"

She pulled a face. "Morris dancing."

Carmen sniggered.

Aggie took his arm and they headed up to the house.

Chapter Six
The Village Fayre

At dinner that evening, Snowy rubbed against Mrs. Euston's shins in delight when she gave him the kippers from Aggie's house, but a short while later, he ran upstairs, tail twitching in disgust.

Billy followed. He found his new friend pacing on the bedroom carpet.

"Twice a day," Snowy moaned. "How am I supposed to survive if they only feed me twice a day?"

"You'll be fine. My dad bought plenty of dry cat food home for you. He says you can have it whenever you want."

"Very nice I'm sure, but cats need proper nourishment."

"Of course you do," Billy sat on his bed. "But my dad *is* a vet. He knows about this sort of thing." Snowy gave him a haughty look. "Oh sure, a vet's bound to know more than me. After all, I'm just a cat. What would I know about feline feeding requirements?"

"I don't see why you're making such a fuss. We both know you'll just go around the village, scrounging food from everybody like you always do."

Snowy stopped pacing and sat down. "Well, maybe," he said, "but it's the principle of the thing."

Billy changed the subject. "Listen, I found out

something about this 'Fur-Face' today. We need to meet up with Razor."

"We can't. You promised your dad you wouldn't leave the house at night, remember?"

A sly grin spread across Billy's face. "True, but he didn't say not to go down to the kitchen. Do you think Razor could get in through the cat flap."

"A bloody great horse could get in through the hole your dad put in the door."

"Good. You can wait for him outside. When he turns up, bring him into the kitchen, then come and wake me up."

Snowy lifted his right foreleg in mock salute. "Yes, your bleedin' highness. Would you like me to bring you a cup of tea while I'm at it?"

"Sorry. I didn't mean to make it sound like an order."

"Doesn't matter anyway. Razor won't put his nose inside a human house, no matter how much he wants news of his family. Just give me a message, I can pass it on for you."

"I wish I could, but I really need to look at his head." Billy sighed. "I suppose we'll just have to be extra careful."

Six hours later, Billy stood at the bottom of the garden. Thick clouds obscured the moon. He could barely make out his hand, even when he held it in front of his nose. He had his torch, but the batteries were all but drained so he wanted to save it for when Razor showed up.

Snowy had wandered off somewhere.

Alone in the darkness, Billy began to have second thoughts. Out here in the dark, his imagination worked overtime. He took slow, deep breaths to calm his nerves.

A sharp hiss came from somewhere close by, above and behind him, followed a moment later by an eerie, rustling sound.

Billy's heart cannoned around inside his chest as he peered into the blackness. More noises came from somewhere overhead. KERRUNCH. CRUNCH. SLIRRUP. CRUNCH.

He fumbled for the torch. "Snowy?" he whispered. "Is that you?"

No answer.

The weak light was little better than a candle, but it pushed back the darkness enough to reveal Snowy, sprawled on the shed roof alongside an open packet of crispy snacks. On the other side of him, a bottle of cola, with one of Emma's bendy straws sticking out of it.

The cat took another long drink. SLIRRUP! "Ah, that hits the spot." He grinned at Billy. "Fancy a drop?"

Billy scowled. "No I do not. You nearly gave me a heart attack. Why didn't you answer me?"

"My mouth was full. It would have been rude."

Before Billy could reply, Razor trotted out from the bushes. "Did you find them?"

"Not yet." He told Razor all about his conversation with Professor Sedgewick. "If the one you called 'Gallstone' is really Gladstone, then Aggie sent them packing months ago. They aren't supposed to be there. They must have got back in somehow, to carry on their work in secret. I think Scala and your cubs are still at the research compound. We need to find a way to get a look

71

inside."

"Couldn't your dad get you in?" Snowy asked, from on top of the shed.

"I don't think so. Dad's the chief surgeon, but he's based at *Adventure Safari*. He's not involved with the research side."

Snowy thought for a moment. "Maybe you could ask old Marcus for a guided tour. He's a bit of a twit, but he's a decent bloke."

"I don't know," Billy said. "He doesn't seem the 'guided tour' sort. Still, there's no harm in trying. I can ask tomorrow, at the Summer Fayre."

"You should invite Carmen along," Snowy said. "You know, make a date of it."

Billy couldn't see him but he knew the cat was grinning.

Snowy began to sing. "And when two lovebirds coo-ah, they still say Howdee do-ah."

"She's not my girlfriend." He crouched in front of Razor. "Yesterday, you said Fur-Face shaved your head. May I take a look?"

Razor nodded.

Billy removed the helmet. He tried to examine the fox's head with one hand, while holding the torch in the other. "It's no good. Your fur's grown back. I can't see the skin. I need two hands."

"Never fear, Snowy's here." The cat jumped down from the shed to take Billy's torch in his front paws.

"That's better, thanks." Billy parted the fur on Razor's head. He found what he was looking for behind the left ear. "Just as I expected."

"What is it?" Razor asked.

"I think Fur-Face put a microchip in your head to help you understand humans. I found a small scar, just here," he touched Razor's ear. "Snowy has one in the same place."

"And a few others," Snowy added.

"That explains why he shaved your head. Farofas kept his experiments secret. Aggie would never have allowed this kind of thing. I'm sorry."

"But what has he done with my family?"

Billy sat against the shed door. "I think they're in the compound with the other animals. The rest of the scientists would assume they're for use in the proper communication research."

The light of the torch reflected off Razor's eyes as he looked up. "What?"

"Don't worry, my dad says Professor Sedgewick loves animals. I don't think they're in any immediate danger."

Before Razor could answer, the upper half of the back yard lit up.

"It's your dad," Snowy said. "He's at your bedroom window."

The light from the house didn't quite reach the shed. Billy slipped the torch into his trouser pocket and drew his knees up to his chest, praying his father couldn't see him. "If he catches me outside after I promised…"

The bedroom light went out. The moon emerged from behind the clouds, casting an eerie glow over the back yard.

Snowy squinted at the house. "Crafty beggar. He came back to the window. I think he wants to catch you in the act."

"What do I do now?" Billy looked about him, as if expecting to find the answer amongst the flowerbeds. "I'll be grounded for sure."

"Hang on," Snowy said. "I've got an idea." He gestured to the back of the house. "Razor, see that hole in the kitchen door? When I give the word, head toward it."

"You want me to enter a human house?"

"Of course not." Snowy looked at the silhouette in the window. "We just need his dad to think you will. Leave your helmet here."

"I don't understand–"

"You don't have to. You asked for Bill's help, now he needs yours. When we're ready, trot up the path toward the back door, then get out of the way, 'cause Bill and I will be coming in fast."

"But I can't go back inside now," Billy said. "Not with my dad watching."

Snowy jumped onto the water barrel. "Don't worry, kid. I have a plan…and it's so crazy, it might just work."

From his vantage point at the window, Dr. Euston squinted through the darkness at the bottom of the yard. "You're out there somewhere, Billy Euston." He muttered. Then Snowy stepped out from the shadows.

"I knew it."

A moment later, a fox appeared. Dr. Euston looked on in horror, expecting it to pounce on the unsuspecting cat, but, to his amazement, it stood right next to Snowy for at least thirty seconds, then trotted up the garden path to the back door.

"The cat flap!"

He sprinted out of the room, catching his knee on the doorframe as he went. With a loud yelp he tumbled to the hall floor. Ignoring the pain, he staggered to his feet, determined to reach the kitchen before the fox came inside. Halfway down the stairs he heard a loud crash, as something heavy hit the back door. Moments later, he limped into the kitchen to find Billy, standing over the cat flap in the back door with a metal saucepan in his hands.

"You all right, Dad? I heard a noise upstairs."

"Never mind that." Dr. Euston shifted his weight to his uninjured leg. "I told you not to go outside at night."

Billy stared back at him with an overly-innocent expression. "Outside? In my jockey shorts?"

Dr. Euston noticed his son's lack of clothing.

Billy held up the pan. "A fox just poked its head inside. It ran off when I threw this."

"I saw it in the garden," Dr. Euston hobbled to the fridge to get some ice. "It walked right up to Snowy, but didn't attack." He shook his head. "It was the weirdest thing. It seemed like they knew each other. All the same, best call him inside. I'll fit one of those lockable cat flaps tomorrow. Snowy will have to stay inside at night from now on."

"He's been here with me the whole time." Billy nodded across the room to where Snowy sat beneath the kitchen table, slurping a bowl of milk. "He kept pestering me for a drink, so I brought him down here."

While Billy stacked boxes of laundry powder in front of the cat flap, Dr. Euston looked from Snowy, to the back door, then back at Snowy. "But he... I could have sworn..." He wrapped the crushed ice in a tea towel, then winced as he applied it to his swollen knee.

"Why are you two out of bed? And what was that banging?" Mrs. Euston frowned at them from the staircase.

Dr. Euston lifted the makeshift icepack to show off his injury. "I fell over."

"Serves you right," his wife scolded. "You shouldn't have been up in the first place."

"But–"

"No buts. Off to bed, the pair of you." She marched back up the stairs. "Honestly, I sometimes think I'm the only grownup in this house."

Without another word, they hurried after her.

Snowy finished his milk before going upstairs. He padded across the bedroom carpet and half-jumped, half-clambered onto Billy's bed. "Told you it would work," he whispered. "Lucky for us we haven't had rain for a while, you'd have had a tough job explaining muddy footprints all over the kitchen floor."

Billy scratched the top of his friend's head. "First thing tomorrow, I'll sneak out to collect my clothes from behind the shed. Thanks, I owe you one."

The next morning, Mrs. Euston announced a new family tradition. "Your father and I decided we should start going to church. We can meet some of our new neighbors."

They were nearly late. The congregation, which seemed to include the entire village, had already begun to sing the opening hymn as the Eustons took their seats.

Billy had never been in an old church before. He

noticed the smell first, a mixture of dusty stone, candle wax and furniture polish. Seating came in the form of long pews. Little more than elongated wooden benches, made of dark, weathered wood, each pew had room for a dozen people. Set out in neat rows, facing forward, a six-foot gap between them ran the length of the church. A white lace cloth covered the altar, on top of which sat a heavy gold cross.

Billy stood between his mother and Emma, who made a great show of reading from her upside-down hymn-book. Unfamiliar with the tune, he pretended to sing along with the congregation, mouthing the words as he gazed around him. Helen (or perhaps, Penny) Roberts sat to the left of the altar, playing the organ. Marcus Sedgewick stood next to her with the rest of the choir.

A kaleidoscope of colors streamed through the arched windows which ran along either side of the church. Centuries old, the windows sat high in the walls, each frame filled with small pieces of colored glass, cleverly arranged to depict a scene from the bible. The nearest one showed Noah, welcoming animals aboard the Ark. Beneath it, Billy saw a small bronze plaque. Time and decades of polishing had worn away the inscription. From this distance, all he could make out was the year: 1724.

The hymn came to an end. From the bench behind him, Billy picked up a bright blue cushion with an image of a golden cross woven into the cover. He went to sit on it, but his mother stopped him. "That's for kneeling on."

Red-faced, he pushed the cushion onto the concrete floor and sat.

At the altar, the vicar began his sermon. A stout, friendly-looking man with very little hair and large, bushy eyebrows, The Reverend Loampit wore a white, cotton surplice over a plain, black cassock. The surplice reminded Billy of the vinyl poncho Emma wore when painting.

The combination of Loampit's monotone delivery and the acoustic echoes of the church's interior made it hard to concentrate. He found himself staring at the tips of Loampit's well-polished, but mispaired shoes, one black, one brown, which poked out from beneath the frayed edges of the the vicar's ankle-length cassock.

As the sermon went on, Billy looked for a familiar face in the crowded church. He spotted Carmen, distinctive in a bright pink top, sitting with Aggie in the front row, but though he recognized some of his immediate neighbors, he saw no other children his age.

During the service, Reverend Loampit called the Eustons to the front of the church, where he officially introduced them to the village. The vicar had obviously done his research, because he gestured to Billy and Emma, announcing his delight at having a worm collector and a budding young writer join his flock. "In case you're wondering, Emma is the worm collector."

Everyone laughed.

Except Billy, who shot an accusing glance at Carmen. She stared back at him and shook her head. He turned to his mother, but she had her hands full, trying to keep Emma from banging at the keys on the church organ. "Mom," he hissed, as they trooped back to their seats.

"I'm sorry," she whispered. "He asked about you

both in the store the other day. I didn't know he'd say anything here."

After the service, Billy hung around outside the church, playing games on his otherwise useless cell phone, while his parents chatted with the locals. He felt a hand on his shoulder and turned to see the Reverend Loampit standing there, with a concerned look on his face.

"I saw you blush earlier," Loampit said. "I didn't mean to embarrass you, lad."

Billy shrugged.

"You know, son, your mother looked so proud when she told me about your writing, I assumed you'd be too." Loampit grinned. "What is it they say now? 'Never assume, in case you make an 'ASS' out of 'U' and 'ME'." The vicar brushed an insect from his white, cotton surplice. "My childhood is long behind me. I'd forgotten how much of an embarrassment mothers and vicars can cause even when they don't mean to. Can you forgive an old fool an honest mistake?"

Billy couldn't help smiling. He took Loampit's outstretched hand, "Of course, but please don't do it again."

"You have my word. Now, tell me all about this new superhero of yours. During the week, I'll see if I can't dig out some of my old comic books for you to look at. It might surprise you to learn that even old codgers like me used to read them."

A few minutes later, Billy spotted Carmen and Aggie, chatting with his parents. He sidled over to them.

"I don't know how old Lump-it found out about your comics," Carmen said, "but I didn't tell him, honest."

"I know; my mom did." Billy fished inside his trouser pocket and pulled out a box of Tic Tacs. He offered one to Carmen. "The vicar's nice though. He apologized."

Carmen shook a couple of mints into her hand. "They're all nice really. They're just so…boring. I've spent every summer break here for the last seven years. Nothing interesting ever happens." He must have pulled a face because she added. "Don't get me wrong, I'm glad I've met you. I'd go insane if I got stuck here on my own all summer. At least the weather stayed fine for the Summer Fayre."

"Do you have to work at one of the exhibits?"

Carmen tossed the mints in the air and caught them in her mouth, one after the other. "I'm not Morris-dancing, if that's what you mean."

They both laughed.

"Helen wants me to help run the tombola. Aggie's doing one of the displays. I don't know which one. What about you?"

"I might help my dad on the theme park stand, but only for a little while." Billy grinned. "I don't want to miss Professor Sedgewick's dance troupe."

Carmen wagged a finger at him. "Don't laugh. In a few years, they'll want you on the village team."

Bright, glorious sunshine beamed down on Little Chumberry's annual Summer Fayre. Wooden stalls and colored tents lined the outer edge of the village green. Delighted squeals and the excited chatter of hundreds of visitors filled the air. Rock music boomed out over the public address system. The smell of freshly-cut grass mingled with the mouth-watering aroma of hot dogs, fried onions and other food from the refreshment stands.

For the first part of the afternoon, Billy helped his father on the *Adventure Safari* stand. They sold books and animal toys donated by the park. In the space next to them, Mrs. Euston sat with Emma as she helped Penny Roberts on the face-painting stall, where an endless procession of small children hopped about in varying degrees of impatience as they waited to be transformed into their favorite jungle animal. The older ones ran from one stall to the next, as if worried the Fayre might vanish before they'd seen everything.

Adult visitors strolled around the green at a more sedate pace, inspecting the exhibitions, like the ones for old-style metal-craft and glass-blown products. Long lines snaked out from the hot dog stands and the ice cream van. On the far side of the green, people tried their luck at throwing horseshoes, or any one of a host of other fun things to do and see.

After about an hour, Billy collected Carmen from her post on the tombola and together they explored the Fayre, enjoying the displays and playing games like 'Whack-The-Rat' or 'Find-The-Nail'.

At four o'clock, the church bells signaled the afternoon entertainment to begin. A group of brightly-colored clowns appeared. Amid much falling over and water-squirting from plastic flowers, they cordoned off the green with a ring of yellow tape to provide a space for the various performers.

The crowd laughed and cheered at the comedy juggling team from the next village. Even Professor

Sedgewick's Morris-dancers received enthusiastic applause, but the audience reserved their greatest appreciation for the motorcycle stunt rider, by far the star act of the show. After a few clever tricks, like riding up and down in front of the audience on just one wheel, four of the clowns drove a battered, yellow car out into the center of the green. They set up jump ramps on either side, with seven-foot hoops at the top of each one. The PA announcer called for silence. The smallest clown set the hoops on fire, while the stunt rider rode a little way off to prepare for the jump.

The crowd held its collective breath. The rider revved the motorbike's engine, then, like a rampaging metal bull, it thundered across the grass at a terrific pace.

Billy watched in awe as it went up the ramp and through the first ring of fire. Flames reached after the bike as it sailed over the car. The motorcycle's back wheel clipped the second burning hoop as it went through. The fiery circle wobbled, but did not fall. A moment later, bike and rider landed safely on the other ramp.

Everyone cheered as the stunt rider rode around in a wide circle, waving to the spectators.

When the announcer asked for the rider to take a final bow, the crowd stood in stunned silence for a moment, then gave a roar of delight. For when the helmet came off, they saw Aggie's smiling face, beaming back at them.

Billy shook his head in wonder. "Now I know why they call her Daft Aggie."

While members of the village fire service doused

the flames, the clowns cleared everything away, then set up a small platform where the car had been. It was time for the afternoon announcements. There were competitions for the strangest things. Apart from various cake and jam-making prizes, there were awards for things like, 'biggest marrow', or ' juiciest tomato'. Penny Roberts won something in the 'Rude Shaped Vegetable' competition.

The village school children had planted sunflower seeds in class the previous month. Aggie awarded a big tin of chocolates for the one which had grown the tallest. After the awards, the visitors drifted away, leaving the villagers to tidy up.

Billy wandered around with a large garbage sack, collecting empty soda cans, discarded paper napkins and other rubbish. On the other side of the green he spotted Professor Sedgewick helping several of the Morris-dancing team fold up the marquee.

Now's my chance to ask him for a tour.

Marcus looked up as Billy approached. "Enjoy the Fayre?"

"Oh yes, Aggie was amazing. I loved those jugglers." He glanced at Marcus's outfit, then quickly added, "I enjoyed your dance group too."

"Yeah, right." Marcus stretched his back. "Let's face it. It may be a centuries-old tradition, but if the England rugby team tried Morris-dancing before the next international, it would hardly terrify the opposition."

Billy laughed. "I suppose not. So why do it?"

"It's part of our heritage. Morris dancing has been going on since before Shakespeare's time. Also," Marcus lowered his voice and gave him a sheepish grin, "I thought it might help me fit in around here."

Marcus put his hands behind his back and stretched again. "You know, your dad's been here less than a week, and he already seems to know everyone's name. The locals treat him as if he's lived here all his life. I've been here since last October, yet I still feel like an outsider." He sighed. "I've never been good with people."

Billy picked up an empty coke bottle. "I know how you feel. Maybe you try too hard. Dad always says 'Treat everyone the same, but treat them right.' It seems to work for him."

They strolled across the grass toward the beer tent. "How about you?" Marcus asked. "Don't you miss all your London friends?"

Billy thought for a moment before answering. "To be honest, I never had many. I liked different things to the other kids. Most of them found me a bit odd."

"Because you write comic books? I thought kids *loved* comics. I know I did at your age."

Billy laughed. "You didn't have so many video games back then." He couldn't bring himself to ask for the tour. It doesn't feel right, he thought, I'd be taking advantage.

Carmen joined them. "Aggie's invited everyone back to her place for a late night supper. Your mom took Emma home, but your dad says you can go along with him if you like. Do you want to come?"

"My first village party? Of course. How about you, Professor?"

Professor Sedgewick grinned. "Call me Marcus. And you know what, I think I will."

Billy and his father didn't get home till after midnight. Not wanting to disturb the rest of the family, they kept the lights off. Billy cleaned his teeth in the kitchen sink and made his way upstairs. He wanted to talk to Snowy, but in the dim light he could see him curled on the bed, fast asleep.

He fumbled under his pillow for his pajamas, changed, then climbed under the duvet, careful not to wake Snowy. For a long time, he lay on his back with his hands behind his head, thinking. He wished he'd taken his chance to ask Marcus for a tour of the center. No sense crying over spilt milk, he thought.

The next time I see him, I'll ask. If not, I'll have to find another way to get inside the research center.

He drifted off to sleep and dreamed of Morris-dancing clowns, jumping through burning hoops.

Chapter Seven
Operation 'Vetstipal'

Billy awoke to the distant ringing of the telephone, followed by the muffled sound of his mother's voice and her footsteps on the stairs.

She knocked on his bedroom door and came in. "Billy, you have a phone– " Her jaw dropped. "What on earth happened in here?"

He sat up, bleary-eyed. "Nothing, Mom, I..."

His voice trailed away. The room looked as if a tornado had passed through it. Apart from the area between the door and his bed, the floor was a chaotic jumble of CDs and empty food wrappers. His DVD collection now lay beneath the window, the discs piled in an untidy heap beside their cases. The dark-green carpet appeared to be crawling with little yellow insects which, on closer inspection, he realized were actually biscuit crumbs.

Empty cola bottles lay clustered together around the wastebasket. In the middle of the room, the TV remote and an empty box of microwave popcorn rested against one of his mother's favorite cushions, which was covered in cat hair and now had an unpleasant-looking stain on one corner.

With a groan, Billy flopped his head back onto the pillow.

"Oh no you don't." His mother yanked off the bedcovers. "Get yourself out of bed and clean up this pigsty right now. I've never seen such a mess." She snatched up the cushion and shook it at him. "There'll be no breakfast for you until this place is spotless. I'll tell Carmen you'll have to ring her back." Without waiting for a reply, she marched out of the room.

Billy clenched his eyes shut for a second, but when he opened them again, the room hadn't changed. "I'm going to kill that cat." He stumbled out of bed, crushing a half-eaten custard cream beneath his foot on the way to the door.

After a quick shower, he got dressed and set to work. Most of the CDs had to be wiped clean before he put them back in their proper cases. The DVD collection had fared no better. When he finished clearing them away, he filled the wastebasket with as much rubbish as he could pick up with his fingers, then went over the carpet with the vacuum cleaner.

"Here comes the party animal," his father said, when Billy finally made it to the kitchen. "What's this I hear about you carrying on the party in your room last night? And more importantly, why wasn't I invited?" His smile vanished when he saw the expression on his wife's face. "I mean, it's not good, son. Your mother said it looked like we'd been burgled."

"Sorry about all the mess. I could hardly believe it myself."

Snowy stepped into the kitchen through the cat flap in the back door, humming a tune. "Morning, all."

Billy glowered at him, but Snowy strolled off into the front room without meeting his gaze.

Dr. Euston watched him go, then took a sip of coffee. "You also need to think about poor Snowy. Cats are very tidy animals you know. They don't like a lot of mess."

His father flung himself backward to avoid the shower of milk which sprayed from Billy's mouth.

Mrs. Euston grabbed a tea towel and mopped up the table. "What is the matter with you today?"

"It went down the wrong way," Billy spluttered. He wiped himself down, then got on with his cereal.

After breakfast, he went in search of Snowy, but couldn't find him. Then he remembered his telephone message and rang Carmen.

"Do you mind if I come and visit this afternoon?" she asked. "I've got a surprise for you."

After lunch, she arrived at the front door with a large envelope in one hand and a crash helmet in the other. She waved to Aggie, who had brought her over on the back of her motorbike.

"I still can't believe she did that stunt yesterday," Billy said.

They went into the kitchen to get a drink. Billy filled two glasses at the sink. In the back yard, Emma helped her mother clear weeds from the vegetable patch, though she seemed more interested in collecting worms. Out of sight of the others, Snowy sprawled out on the shed roof. By his side, a packet of crispy snacks and a cola bottle, with a straw sticking out of it. He had something on his face. "He'd better not break my sunglasses."

"What did you say?" Carmen asked.

"Oh, nothing."

They took their drinks into the dining room, where she handed him the envelope. "For you."

The envelope contained a sketchpad. Billy flicked through the pages. Each sheet contained several, skilled drawings of a masked man with a cape, standing in various tough guy poses. He recognized the colors and markings on the character's superhero outfit. "This is Static-Man. Did you draw these?"

"Do you like them? I hope the colors are okay. I did them yesterday, after church."

Billy sighed "I wish I could draw like this. When I try, he ends up all skinny and out of proportion."

"Good drawing is mostly about getting the basics right," Carmen said. "Anybody can do it, with practice. I can show you, if you like."

He spent the rest of the afternoon sketching and coloring under Carmen's tuition. She certainly knew what she was doing, because by the time Aggie came to take her home, his drawing skills had dramatically improved.

"Why don't you come over to Aggie's tomorrow?" Carmen said. "I can teach you some more about depth perspective and show you the computer software I told you about. Maybe your parents can get it for you."

"I can't. I have to go into town. My Mom wants to take Emma for a haircut."

Aggie, chatting nearby with Mrs. Euston, overheard. "Louise, the Land Rover's in for a service at the moment, but I could collect Billy on the bike. I can fetch him back home after tea. That is," she added, with a mischievous grin, "as long as he promises to leave my place as tidy as he finds it."

Later that evening, Billy went to his bedroom. He didn't feel like watching TV, so he lay on his bed, reading.

Snowy poked his head around the door. "Can I come in?"

Billy didn't look up. "I wondered when you'd show up. You got me in a lot of trouble today."

Snowy sat in the middle of the room. After a long silence he asked, "Good book is it? What's it called?"

"*Henry Porter and the Saucer of Bones*. Don't change the subject. Why did you trash my room?"

"I didn't trash it," Snowy said, "at least, not on purpose. I got bored. You all went out and left me." He jumped onto the windowsill. "I played a few CDs, but your musical taste is a little contemporary for my liking, so I watched a couple of movies. I didn't mean any harm."

"What about all the food on the floor?"

"I felt a little peckish, so I had a snack. I admit, I may have dropped the odd crumb on the carpet, but let's face it, I could hardly carry the vacuum cleaner up the stairs by myself, could I?"

Billy snapped his book shut, losing his place. "Snowy, I found five empty coke bottles in here. Mom had to get some more from the village shop. She thinks I drank it all."

"Come on, you know how crispy snacks make me thirsty."

"This isn't funny. You can't keep doing this. Someone's bound to find out. Besides," Billy added, "it's not fair on me."

Snowy looked quite taken aback. He came over to the bed. "Look, I'm sorry about the mess, okay? I'll try to be more tidy from now on, I promise. I tell you what. Let me make it up to you. What can I do? Just say the word and I'll do it. Would you like to see me juggle some bottle tops?"

"You can juggle?"

"No, but I can give it a try if it'll cheer you up."

Billy couldn't help laughing. "Never mind. I need to find a way inside the research compound. I chickened out of asking Marcus for a tour. Now I have no idea what to do."

When Snowy didn't answer, he went back to his reading, but a short while later, a black paw appeared on top of the page. When he lowered the book, Snowy moved in close. He could smell cheese and onion crispy snacks on the cat's breath. "You said the research center doubles as a vetstipal, right?"

"Yes. Why?"

"And you've arranged to see your pal, Carmen, at Aggie's place tomorrow afternoon, right?"

"Yes, so what?"

Snowy grinned. "Then leave it me. Tomorrow afternoon, we're going in."

Billy had never ridden on the back of a motorcycle before. After Aggie's display at the Summer Fayre, his mother had been a little nervous about it, but Aggie assured her she would take great care.

The moment he donned the crash helmet, Billy lost himself in a wonderful daydream. He imagined himself as a stunt rider, racing through the streets on a movie set.

He felt quite disappointed when the bike came to a halt and he opened his eyes to find he'd already arrived at Aggie's house.

For the next hour, he sat with Carmen while she demonstrated the computer software she used for designing new outfits. He showed her the practice drawings he'd made the previous night, then spent another hour learning all about 3D perspective, and how to draw it.

At four o'clock, Snowy appeared on the patio, waving his front legs in the air to get his attention. Their eyes met and the cat gave him the feline equivalent of a thumbs up.

"Oh look," Billy said, in a loud voice. "There's old Snowy. I wonder what he's up to."

Carmen watched as the cat played out a moving death scene on the back lawn. "Who does he expect to fool with that old trick? Look at him, staggering about on his hind legs with his front paws at his throat. Well I'm not falling for it." She went back to her drawing.

Snowy stopped pretending to choke and trotted across the grass to the side of the lawn.

Billy gestured for him to try something else "Yes, he seems okay now, but why's he climbed up on the greenhouse? I hope he doesn't fall."

This time Carmen didn't even look up. "I shouldn't worry, cats have amazing reflexes. They can fall quite a long way and land as lightly as if they'd just stepped off a small chair."

Out in the back yard, Snowy lost his footing, He slithered backward down the glass roof, then fell off the edge to land with a crash amidst the metal compost bins below.

"Oh yes," Billy said. "Amazing."

Snowy emerged from one of the bins, looking disheveled and slightly dazed. He had dried grass (and what Billy hoped was just mud) splattered across the top of his head. He looked at the house, then spat a lump of something out of his mouth.

Billy tried not to laugh.

Snowy shook his head, then disentangled himself from the mess. He trotted onto the middle of the lawn, where he sat on the grass and threw up his front paws in a 'what do I do now?' gesture.

Billy shrugged. He had no idea.

Snowy sat for a while, staring at the glass doors, then his shoulders slumped. He waved his front paws at Carmen, signaling for Billy to try again, then ran toward them, picking up speed at a surprising rate.

"Honestly, Carmen, can you see what that daft cat is up to now?"

She turned to look, just as Snowy reached the stone patio. A few feet from the back of the house, he sprang into the air. Billy and Carmen both winced when he crashed into sliding glass door. He seemed to hang in mid-air for a moment, about four feet above the ground, his limbs splayed outwards and his face squashed against the glass. With a loud squeaking noise, he slid down.

"Oh my goodness." Carmen leapt out of her chair. She opened the door and crouched over the semi-conscious cat. "Snowy, are you all right? I think he's hurt."

Carmen fetched a large flower basket and Billy lay

Snowy inside. Together, they ran through the garden to the animal surgery at the research compound. At first, Billy thought Snowy might have really injured himself, but as they passed the stables the cat raised a front leg and put the back of his paw against his forehead.

"Oh the pain, the pain. I see a tunnel, with a bright light at the end of it."

"Lie still," Billy hissed. "Don't overdo it."

Snowy winked, then lay back, as if unconscious.

At the research compound they hurried to the stern-looking man at the front desk.

"Please help," Billy tried to sound convincing. "My cat's hurt, he needs to see a vet."

The security guard seemed not to hear. He sniffed the air with distaste, then looked around the main hall, as if searching for the source of an unpleasant odor. His gaze finally came to rest on Snowy's motionless body. "Sorry, kid," he said, in a bored voice. "The surgery's only used on exhibits from *Adventure Safari*. We don't treat common animals here."

Snowy lifted his head. "Common?"

Billy shoved him back down. "The poor thing's having convulsions. He needs help now. He might die!"

The guard folded his arms across his chest. "Not my problem. I don't make the rules. Sorry, kid, you'll just have to find a regular vet."

Billy opened his mouth to argue but, to his surprise, Carmen burst into tears. She flung herself on his shoulder. "I…love…this…cat…" she stammered, between sobs. "If anything happened…to him…I don't know what I'd do."

The guard fingered his collar. "Now then, love,

don't cry." He handed her a few tissues from the box by his phone. "Tell you what. You see those double-doors at the end of the hall? Go through them and on down the stairs to the surgery. I'll ring ahead and get Doctor Morton to have a look at him, as a favor to me."

"Thank you," Carmen said, in a tiny voice. "You're a very kind man." She blew her nose.

As they hurried down the long corridor to the stairs, Billy whispered, "You okay?"

"Of course." Carmen grinned at him from behind her tissue. "You men are so gullible."

"I've always liked her," the 'unconscious' Snowy said through the side of his mouth.

A young vet waited for them at the bottom of the stairs. "I'm Doctor Morton, I hear you've an injured cat needs seeing to."

Billy explained what happened as they followed him through the double-doors into the surgery.

"Best if you wait here," Doctor Morton said, indicating some chairs. "I need to give him a thorough examination. Don't worry, we'll look after him." He took the basket and hurried through another set of doors on the opposite side of the room.

So far so good, Billy thought. He wandered around the room, but saw nothing about any research animals.

Voices came from behind the double doors. "Right then, let's have a look at you."

A woman asked, "Isn't that Snowy? What happened to him?"

"Jim Euston's son brought him in with Aggie's granddaughter. They said he ran straight into a glass window. Judging by the smell, I reckon he went through some manure along on the way. He seems okay, but he may have a concussion. If nothing else, he definitely needs a bath. Warm up the shower-tap, Jenny."

"WHAT?"

Billy heard the sound of running water.

"HEY! Stay away from me with that thing. Bill, a little help here please…"

"Hold him steady, nurse, while I add the shampoo."

"Shampoo? I don't think so, mate... BILLY!"

"All right, Snowy, here we go. This won't hurt, I promise. It's only a bit of water and some special soap."

"Then lather yourself up with it. I'm not kidding, I'll stick that soap up your–*arbleubblubblubble*."

After a few seconds, the vet spoke again. "Much better. Hand me a towel please. We've got the worst out of his fur, but he may need another bath later."

"Don't even think about it, pal. When I get home I'm calling my lawyer, or better yet, the Cat Protection League."

Hurried footsteps sounded on the stairs outside.

Professor Sedgewick entered. "Hello, you two. What's up?"

At the same moment, Doctor Morton returned. "You can see him now."

Billy followed Carmen and Marcus into the surgery. Snowy lay on the examination table, wrapped in a cream-colored blanket. He looked wet, but a lot cleaner. Billy dried him while Doctor Morton explained the situation to Marcus.

"It's all right, David," Marcus said. "You did the right thing. Besides, Snowy's practically one of the family, aren't you, boy." He reached out to ruffle

Snowy's matted, wet fur, but snatched his hand back when he saw the look in the cat's eyes. "Well, he seems fine, but we should probably keep him here for a day or so, just to be sure." He scratched at his beard, then asked, "Since you're both here, and if you wouldn't find it too boring, would you like a quick tour?"

Billy couldn't believe his luck. "Really? That would be great."

Marcus laughed. "I meant to ask you last night, after the Summer Fayre, but then I thought, why would a lad like Billy be interested in our research? Dr. Morton will look after old Snowy. You can collect him in a couple of days."

Billy felt a sudden twinge of guilt. "What about his food?"

"We have all the healthy grub a young cat would need," Doctor Morton said. "Don't worry, I'll make sure he doesn't eat too much."

Billy didn't know if that kind of language was appropriate for a nice cat. He knew for certain his mother wouldn't approve, so he pretended not to hear what Snowy shouted after him, as he followed Marcus and Carmen through the double doors.

In truth, the tour proved to be of no help.

An hour after leaving Snowy, they ended up in Marcus's office. "Do you have any other animals here?" Billy asked. "Only, we didn't see Mr. Tinkles."

"Oh, he went back to the infirmary at *Adventure Safari* this morning. If they hadn't been refitting the park's main surgery the other day, your dad wouldn't have brought Mr. Tinkles over here for his operation. Don't worry, he'll be as good as new in no time."

Billy's heart sank. "Only, I thought you might have some non-zoo animals here too. "You know, mice, rats, or even foxes."

Marcus laughed. "Sorry, all we've got are two apes and about thirty monkeys." He glanced at his watch. "I should get back to work. Let me see you to the entrance."

Later, as he sat at Aggie's dinner table, savoring the delicious aroma from the roast dinner Helen had cooked, Billy felt a little guilty about enjoying such a wonderful meal while poor Snowy had to make do with a 'vetstipal' diet for the next two days. Then he remembered the state his room had been in the previous morning and suddenly felt rather hungry.

Chapter Eight
Adventure Safari

Dinner at Aggie's was a new experience for Billy. Back in London, the family had eaten at a small table in the kitchen of their cramped, two-bedroom apartment. Their new home had a separate dining room and a much bigger table, but it seemed tiny compared to the beautiful mahogany one stretched out in front of him. His reflection stared back at him through a swirl of polished wood. The thick, heavy plates and engraved cutlery reminded him of the fancy restaurant his father took them to on their last night in London.

"You seem very quiet, Bill," Aggie said. "Everything all right?"

He took another spoonful of delicious, Chicken Noodle soup. "Sorry, I was miles away."

"Don't worry about Snowy. Doctor Morton will look after him." Carmen sat back, looking puzzled. "I wonder what made him run at the patio door."

Aggie chuckled. "Of course, I'm glad he's okay, but I do wish I could have been there to see him slide down the glass. From your description, it must have looked hilarious."

Billy helped himself to a bread roll from the basket on the table. "Whatever else you say about Snowy, he's not boring."

The mood lightened and they enjoyed the rest of the meal.

The Land Rover had returned from its service, so Billy didn't get another ride on the motorbike when Aggie took him home. Carmen came along too. She sat with him in the back.

As Aggie switched on the engine, Helen hurried out onto the driveway to hand Billy a large bowl, covered with a tea towel. "You said you liked my apple-and-cinnamon crumble, so I made you one to take home for the family." Helen went back indoors with his delighted thanks ringing in her ears.

When they reached the house, Aggie came in to speak to Mrs. Euston. "I meant to ask you this afternoon, Louise. I'm taking Carmen to visit *Adventure Safari* tomorrow. Would you and the children like to come too?"

"We'd be delighted."

"It gets pretty hectic in there most days," Aggie warned, "but things calm down a bit by late afternoon. We'll pick you up at about four o'clock and give you the VIP tour."

Billy waved goodbye from the doorway, then went straight to his room. He considered going out to see Razor, but didn't want to risk getting caught by his parents, especially since he only had bad news for the fox. He decided to wait until Snowy came home.

He tried to read his *Henry Porter* book, but couldn't stay focused. He kept thinking about Snowy, all alone in the research center. In the end he put the book aside and lay back with his hands behind his head, trying to make sense out of the day's events. What had become of Scala and the cubs? He imagined their frightened cries as smoke poured into their lair. They must have got out, but what happened after?

He tossed and turned, unable to settle. Could Doctor Farofas still have them? Where had he based himself? Definitely somewhere nearby, or he couldn't keep sending out rats to kill Razor, but where?

"I can't do this on my own." He wished he could go to his mom and dad, or Aggie, even Marcus Sedgewick, but they'd never believe him. Several times over the past two days he'd noticed the concerned glances his parents gave him when they didn't think he was looking. They know something's going on, he thought, but they'd drop me off at the nearest loony bin if I told them about all this. He slipped into a troubled sleep, having come to the unhelpful conclusion that, whatever happened, he was on his own.

The main entrance to *Adventure Safari* lay on the other side of the woods from Aggie's house, about five miles from the village. Billy felt quite important when, instead of driving around the car park to find a space, they drove through a wide entrance marked:

OFFICIAL PARK STAFF ONLY
SORRY, NO VISITORS ALLOWED.

It opened into a wide courtyard, surrounded by green-painted barns and several wooden huts. Aggie parked the Land Rover and they all clambered out.

A tractor chugged past, towing behind it a small trailer, loaded with bales of hay. Around the yard, men and women, dressed in identical green overalls, loaded other trailers with food for the animals. Billy held his breath to avoid the assortment of unfamiliar (and mostly unpleasant) smells from the buckets of fish, oatmeal, vegetables, raw meat and bundles of hay.

"It's always a little busy in the Preparation Area," Aggie said. "Best keep a close eye on Emma."

Aggie led them into one of the huts. "This office," she said, acknowledging the two workers there, "is the focal point for the park's administration. Pauline and Harry go through all our correspondence, staff enquiries and that kind of thing."

She handed a special visitor pass to Billy and gave two more to his mother. "These give you unlimited access to the park. If you work here, each member of your immediate family gets one. I like to keep my people happy."

She led them out through the back of the hut, along a path toward another green building. It was empty, except for a burly security guard behind a desk who stood when they entered.

"Desmond helps guard the bit of *Adventure Safari* most visitors don't get to see." Aggie produced a plastic card from the back pocket of her jeans. She handed it to Desmond, who swiped it through an electronic lock on the side of a door in the back wall.

He returned the card, then spoke into his radio. "Office Entrance, five coming down."

Aggie stepped through and beckoned the others to follow. Much to Billy's surprise, he found himself at the top of a wide, well-lit corridor. It sloped downward. White, ceramic tiles covered the walls and ceiling. It reminded him of the pedestrian tunnels in the London Underground railway. Aggie led them to a row of electronic people carriers, like the ones used to transport luggage at airports. As they walked, the security camera on the wall turned to follow their every move.

Aggie sat in the driving seat of the nearest carrier, and gestured for the others to climb aboard. "I got the idea from Disney World. *Adventure Safari's* spread out over five square miles. It gets pretty crowded topside during the day. These tunnels help the staff get around the park without adding to the congestion, as well as providing access to the animals in case of an emergency."

The carrier hummed into life. The flashing amber light on top of the pole behind the back seat cast a warm glow against the smooth walls as they headed down the tunnel at a little over ten miles an hour.

Billy sat on the back seat, next to Carmen. "This must have taken ages to build."

"About three years," Aggie said. "A lot of the tunnels were already here, we just smartened them up. For example, this used to be the main shaft from an open-cast copper mine. We designed the park's layout to fit over the original passageways."

"Is that safe?" Mrs. Euston asked.

"Of course. We had to fill in a few shafts under some of the new buildings, but I didn't mind. It gave us somewhere to put the earth from the extra tunnels and enlargements we wanted to make."

A few minutes later, the tunnel opened into a wide, dome-shaped hallway, about a hundred yards in diameter. Billy thought it looked like a futuristic shopping center. Around the dome's outer rim several more tunnels branched off in different directions. Thick, glass walls revealed restaurants, shops and various offices, even a bank.

Park staff, in different colored outfits, bustled around in every direction. Some of them wore animal costumes.

"They must get hot in those outfits," Mrs. Euston said, lifting Emma off her lap.

In the middle of the great hall, a huge, concrete pillar rose to the top of the dome-shaped roof, twenty feet above their heads. Near its top, six metal girders spread outward and upward, disappearing into the ceiling.

Billy pointed at them. "I feel like I'm inside a giant umbrella."

They went into one of the restaurants. Billy sat between Carmen and Aggie. "Do all wildlife parks have something like this?"

"Oh no, dear. *Adventure Safari* is the only one of its kind."

"Why is everyone dressed in different colors?" Mrs. Euston asked.

Aggie handed Emma a menu. "We divided the park into different sections, each one with its own theme. See the man wearing blue? He works in the Marine Corner, the one next to him, with the ginger hair, his green outfit means he comes from the Jungle Trek area.

"What about yellow?" Billy asked, pointing at a group of young women on the back of a passing people carrier.

"Desert Creatures," Carmen said, "and the brown is for Creepers and Crawlers. The color scheme above ground matches the uniforms, it helps visitors find their way around."

Billy watched the hustle and bustle going on outside the window. "It seems so busy."

"They're changing shifts. All team members report here at the start of their working day. They travel to and from their assigned areas through the underground system. Mini cameras around the park send pictures to the control center, over there next to the bank. Our security people can see every inch of *Adventure Safari* from here. We don't often get trouble, but if it comes, we can respond quickly."

Billy noticed a chart on the wall. It showed the topside sections of the park, overlaid onto a map of the tunnel system. It looked like a spider web, with each main tunnel linked to its neighbor by connecting passages at the outer end and also about halfway along. It would be easy to get to anywhere in the park without having to come through the central dome. "Strange, one of the tunnels comes up outside the perimeter."

For a moment he thought he'd found a secret entrance to the park, then realized something displayed on a wall map couldn't be much of a secret.

"It leads out to the staff car park," Aggie said.

After lunch, they went up to the surface to continue their tour. In addition to the wildlife on display, each area had fun rides and activities for the younger visitors. Great care had been taken to disguise the larger entertainment structures in a way that didn't spoil the view of the surrounding countryside.

They had a great time. Emma particularly enjoyed watching Carmen squirt Billy with a Splash-Cannon in the Water Court beside the Penguin Pool. The twenty-foot Giraffe Slide in the Jungle Trek area also went down well.

Later, as they strolled around the tiger compound on the outside edge of the park, Aggie came to a sudden stop. "What are those fools up to? Stay back, everyone."

About twenty yards ahead, two men had climbed the outer wooden railings which ran along either side of the path. One of them had a small knife in his hand. He seemed to be trying to cut through the wire fence surrounding the tiger enclosure. The other man kept a wary eye on a hungry-looking tiger which stared at them from a few yards away.

Aggie strode up the path toward them. "Step away from there at once."

Mrs. Euston kept a firm hold on Emma. "Stay close."

"They look mean," Carmen said. "We should get help."

Billy looked around, but saw no one else nearby.

The men climbed back over the fence. They towered over Aggie as she wagged her finger under the nearest man's nose. "Do you have a death wish? What if the tigers got out? If you don't care about your own safety, think about the other guests."

Both men seemed a little bit drunk. The one with the knife flung out his arms in an exaggerated gesture. "This place is bloody boring. We wanted to liven it up a bit, didn't we, Dave?"

Billy thought Dave looked a little embarrassed.

"Come on, Pete," Dave said. He took his friend's arm. "It *was* a bit stupid when you think about it. Let's just go home, eh?"

"Shaddup." Pete jerked free. He snarled at Aggie. "What's it got to do with you anyway? Nosy old cow."

He leaned down until his forehead almost rested against Aggie's.

She slapped him, hard.

Pete staggered backward, clutching the side of his face.

Aggie advanced upon him and jabbed her finger in his chest. "I despise people like you. You think abusing an old lady makes you look like a big man? Big bully more like. Well, you don't scare me."

The look on Pete's face changed from a scowl to an expression of deep nastiness. He stabbed his knife into the wooden fencepost and loomed over Aggie. "You slapped me. Well, let's see how you like it when I slap you back, you nasty old–"

Carmen screamed as Pete raised his hand to strike, but the blow never landed. Instead, the man let out a high-pitched yelp, then froze. For several seconds he stood there, motionless. At first, Billy thought he'd heard Carmen and come to his senses, but the color drained from Pete's face, and eyes bulging, he dropped to his knees, clutching his groin.

Aggie stepped in close. She spoke in a calm voice, as if they were making small talk. "When I was a girl, I lived in Hong Kong. My father decided I should learn how to defend myself, so every morning, for three hours straight, I studied Tai Chi and Chinese Boxing with Master Chen Yeu." She straightened up. "Not every old lady is as helpless as you think. Remember that next time."

Pete opened his mouth, but no sound came out.

Aggie looked at the other man. "You wouldn't pick on a defenseless old lady, would you?"

Dave looked from Aggie to his incapacitated friend. He took a step backwards and shook his head. "Oh no, Miss, not me, Miss."

"I'm glad to hear it. I think, perhaps, it's time you left. Don't you?"

"Good idea. Great idea, Miss."

Heavy footsteps pounded up the path behind them. Billy turned to watch two security guards race toward them. When he looked back, Pete had toppled sideways onto the ground. Some color had returned to the man's cheeks, but he still didn't speak. He lay there, staring at Aggie in disbelief.

She turned to address the approaching guards. "Escort these young men to the main gate. And have someone check on this fence, please. It may be damaged."

The security guards took the troublemakers away.

Aggie sauntered back down the path to rejoin Billy and the others. "All that excitement's made me thirsty. Who fancies a cold drink?"

On the way to the food halls the path split, and Billy, who was still trying to figure out exactly what had just happened, kept on going when he should have turned to the left.

"Not that way," Carmen called out. "Unless you'd rather visit the Local Life section than get a drink."

Billy doubled back. He'd almost caught up with the others, when he stopped in his tracks. "Local Life? Is it for British animals?"

"Oh yes," Aggie said. "Not our most popular

exhibit, but I felt they should be included. After all, they were here first. We opened it a few months ago."

Billy felt excitement bubbling up inside him. "What sort of animals have you got down there?"

"You know, badgers, hedgehogs, stoats, weasels, that kind of thing."

Billy hardly dared ask. "Foxes?"

"Of course."

Billy beamed at her. "You go on. I'd like to see them."

"Me too," Carmen said.

Mrs. Euston gave her son a peculiar look. "Five minutes, no more."

"What's all this about?" Carmen asked, trying to match Billy's pace as he set off down the hill.

"Oh, probably nothing. I just need to check something."

They reached the Local Life section, which seemed quite small compared to the other areas of the park. They hurried along, scanning the notice boards on each exhibit. At the far end, Billy spotted the drawing of a fox on a sign. He broke into a run. Surely they couldn't be here, but it made sense. After all, nobody was looking for them, except Razor of course, but he wouldn't think to look here.

Carmen caught up with him in front of the enclosure. "You must really like foxes."

Instead of answering, he leaned over the wooden rail to get a better view of the kennel-like structure, almost hidden amongst the trees at the far end of the enclosure. At first, he saw no sign of movement, but then a fox came out from behind some bushes with a young cub. They trotted up the ramp into the hut.

"Is it a male or female?" Billy asked.

"The cub's a hint," Carmen said. They don't hang around the males too much."

"So it *is* a vixen," Billy said. "Only one cub though," he added, half to himself.

Carmen pointed at the bushes. "No, over there, look."

Billy followed the line of her finger. Another cub trotted into view. It turned to look at them for a moment, then went into the kennel.

They waited a couple of minutes, but no other foxes appeared.

"There you go. One vixen, two fox cubs. Was it worth the detour?"

"You have no idea." They set off up the hill to rejoin the others. "Your grandmother's one tough lady."

Carmen laughed. "Yes, and you'd better watch out, 'cause it runs in the family. Come on, last one to the hot dog stand buys the soda."

She dashed up the path. Billy chased after her, as fast as he could.

Carmen won by half a yard.

Chapter Nine
"Billy Euston, We Have a Problem"

The moment he walked through his front door, Billy recoiled at the stench of paint and wallpaper glue. Someone had been decorating. He followed his mother upstairs. Through his parents' open bedroom door he saw the contents of his room stacked against the far wall.

He joined his mother in the doorway of his own bedroom. "I appreciate the thought, Jim," she said, "but I thought we agreed I would decorate in here?"

Billy stood on tiptoe to peer over her shoulder into what seemed to be some kind of building site. The ceiling had received a fresh coat of white paint. It looked very clean and had already dried. The rest of his belongings were stacked on the bed, which had been dragged into the middle of the room, then covered with large, cream-colored dustsheets. The carpet had been removed, revealing dusty, wooden floorboards. A red, plastic bucket stood at one end of the pasting table, which had been set up in front of the window.

His father stood halfway up a stepladder in the far corner of the room, brushing out air-bubbles from a strip of wallpaper. Splatter-marks from the ceiling paint covered the sleeves of his faded green sweatshirt. A large blob of glue sat on top of his head like a translucent lump of bubble gum. "Surprise! I met

Marcus for lunch today, I told him I planned to leave early so I could make a start in here. He volunteered to give me a hand. You just missed him." He grinned at Billy. "What do you think, son?"

Billy opted for tact. "Mom's the decorator. You should ask her."

When his parents had first met, and before children came along to command her full-time attention, his mother had been a successful interior designer, as well as a skilled painter and decorator.

"It looks good, Jim," she said. "Although, I usually paint the radiator and woodwork *before* starting on the walls, which aren't very smooth so we should really put up some lining paper first."

His father's face fell.

"But you did a great job on the ceiling," she added, ignoring the large, unpainted area around the bedroom light. "It should look even better after the second coat."

Their eyes met. Dr. Euston sighed. "I'd better tear this down and start clearing up."

Because his room was in such a state, Billy's parents decided he should sleep downstairs on the sofa. He made himself comfortable amongst the cushions and pulled the duvet over himself.

My legs ache, he thought. We must have walked a hundred miles today. Keen to give Razor the good news, he set his alarm clock for shortly after midnight. Unfortunately, as he tucked it under the cushions, he accidentally clicked the 'off' switch. Tired out by the day's long walk, he soon nodded off, and without the alarm to wake him, stayed fast asleep until morning.

* * *

That night, Razor waited at the bottom of the Eustons' garden, hoping for news. He wondered why no one had come out to see him for two nights in a row. He decided to look for Snowy in the back yard of *The Laughing Milkmaid*, but when he reached the pub, he found no sign of him.

Where could they be? He didn't have much faith in the cat's abilities, but the human had seemed quite reliable. Maybe they just haven't found out anything, he thought. I'll come back tomorrow.

He cut across the fields behind the pub and made his way through the wood. The stench of burning cloyed at his throat. Earlier in the day, humans had pulled the overhanging branches from the trees along the edge of the field. They'd disposed of them in two campfires, about a hundred yards apart from each other.

Five hours later, Razor still couldn't smell anything other than charred wood. The smoke had no effect on his ears though, and right now they were telling him something was very wrong.

Foxes have incredible hearing. They can pick up the sound of the smallest animals rustling in the grass, or even under the ground. For a fox, the true art of listening is not so much about what they can hear, but rather, their ability to filter out the noises which aren't important.

Razor stood still and listened to the silence. Normally, he would have picked up the distant sounds of mice and other creatures scurrying out of his path, but now...

He peered into the darkness. To his sharp eyes, it could have been the middle of the day. Everything looked normal.

Then he heard it, a soft 'click' from behind a tree, some twenty feet away. He cocked his head to one side. Had Fur-Face sent another rat? Unlikely, he'd killed one just this morning. Something about the tree didn't look right. His gaze wandered up from the base of the trunk. One of the branches looked out of place. Too straight, not quite natural.

Humans!

He ran.

A dazzling white light flooded the area behind him. As he dashed back up the path, a metal dart brushed past his whiskers and thudded into a nearby tree.

When he reached the open field at the edge of the wood, a car pulled up in his path.

Half-blinded by the bright searchlight mounted on its roof, he veered into the thicket on his left. Sharp thorns clawed at him, tearing the helmet from his head, but he forced his way through the dense foliage. A few moments later, he fought his way clear. He raced off through the trees toward the far end of the wood, away from his pursuers.

After a while he changed direction, and headed to the top of a small hill. Once there, he crouched behind a fallen tree trunk, panting heavily, but ready to run again at the first sign of trouble. While he waited for his night vision to return, he listened for sounds of pursuit, half expecting to hear a dozen humans charging through the undergrowth toward his hiding place, but apart from his own thundering heartbeat, and the anxious chatter of some squirrels in a nearby tree, he heard nothing.

He waited a long time before deciding it was safe, then crawled under a thick bush, where he settled down for a few hours of wary sleep.

At daybreak, he crawled out from his hiding place. I need to find a new lair now, he thought. I'll leave a signal for Scala at our old home, in case she manages to get the cubs out and tries to find me.

He sniffed the air as he approached the scene of the previous night's attack. The smell of burning had all but disappeared now.

The humans had long since gone.

Steering well clear of his current lair, he made his way to the home he'd shared with Scala. A thought occurred to him. Of course! The humans started yesterday's fires to spoil my sense of smell. The fools, don't they know you can't outsmart a fox?

He trotted across the well-trodden grass at the entrance to his old den. The moment his paw crossed the threshold, he heard a sharp hissing sound. From somewhere down the tunnel, a gust of wind hit him in the face. The odor seemed vaguely familiar.

"Oops."

Then everything went black.

"Tea up, son."

Billy opened his eyes to see his father smiling down at him with a mug of hot tea in his hand. The delicious smell of frying bacon prodded the rest of his senses awake.

Billy sipped at his tea while his dad went back into the kitchen. He returned with a tray, laden with food and mugs. He handed Billy his breakfast. "There you go. I made some for your mom too, back in a tick."

Billy took a big bite of his bacon sandwich, then

leaned back on the sofa, trying to remember his weird dream from the night before. He'd been watching a DVD with his father. Bruce Lee had started a fight with Jackie Chan, then Aggie had come along and told them off. He'd turned to ask his dad something, only to find Marcus sitting there, with Razor's metal helmet perched on top of his head.

Razor!

He fumbled under the cushions for his alarm clock. *I didn't switch it on. Poor Razor, I hope he didn't wait too long. I'll apologize tonight. He'll be so pleased to hear we might have found Scala and the cubs, he won't be upset.*

His father came back downstairs. "I've got the day off, so I thought I'd take Emma into town while I sort out your new bedroom carpet. They can deliver it this evening. Then I have to pick up another couple of rolls of wallpaper, and a new electric toothbrush. Mine's looking a bit chewed up. You help your mother finish off your room. When I get back, we can take a stroll over to the research center, to collect Snowy."

The previous evening, Mrs. Euston had painted the skirting board and the other woodwork in Billy's room. The next task was to put up lining paper.

Billy mixed glue in the plastic bucket. His mother papered the walls. By mid-afternoon, they'd finished.

Afterward, while they relaxed at the kitchen table, enjoying a late lunch and a cup of tea. His mother asked, "Who's Razor?"

Billy nearly dropped his mug. "Sorry?"

She fixed him with a piercing stare. "Your dad told me he heard you call out 'Razor' in your sleep the other night. And this morning, you kept muttering his name at the pasting board. Is he one of the villagers?"

Billy stared at his drink.

His mother leaned back in her chair. "I know about your little excursion the other night. Your dad thinks you might be in some kind of trouble."

"What? No, of course not."

Billy stared around the room, desperate to avoid meeting her gaze, but wherever he looked, his eyes felt drawn back to hers.

"To be honest, Bill, we're worried about you. Your father heard you talking to Snowy the other day."

Billy's mouth went completely dry. His hand shook as took a gulp of hot tea. "I'm fine, Mom, really."

"Are you sure? We worry you don't have anyone your own age to be friends with in the village, especially since you didn't want to move here in the first place. We just assumed there'd be some other children around."

"Old Lumpit has a saying about that word." Billy saw his mother's puzzled expression, "I mean, Reverend Loampit has a saying. You don't need to worry about me, honest."

She held his gaze for a long time, then nodded, more to herself than to Billy. "All right, but talk to me if things get you down. Moms make better listeners than cats." She smiled. "You don't need imaginary friends when you've got your parents to turn to."

Just then, the front door opened. Emma ran in from the hall, clutching her new Pretty Pony Arctic Explorer doll. Glad of an excuse to leave the kitchen, Billy hurried outside to help his father bring in the rest of the shopping from the car.

An hour later, leaving Mrs. Euston to supervise the fitting of Billy's new carpet, the rest of the family set off through the village toward the research center.

"I hope they looked after Snowy," Billy said.

"Of course they did, son. Ouch!" Dr. Euston winced as Emma, who sat astride his shoulders, whacked him on the head with her new doll.

"Emmy want horsy back."

"Not 'horsy-back', 'piggy-back'," Dr. Euston corrected her, "and for the eleventh time since we left the house, no. Ow! Stop it."

"Maybe she means Snowy," Billy said. "She called him 'horsy' when we first got him." He looked up at his sister. "Yes, Emma, we'll get horsy back soon."

He wasn't sure she understood, but they reached the entrance to the research center without any further blows to Dr. Euston's head. They found Marcus, waiting for them at the reception desk. He looked relieved to see them.

Dr. Euston pointed to the blood-stained handkerchief, wrapped around the professor's hand. "What happened?"

"Snowy got a bit upset. He er...didn't want to go in the cat box."

Billy felt a surge of panic. "Snowy hates cat boxes. Is he all right?"

They hurried down the corridor toward the stairs. When they reached the lower level, Billy heard a familiar voice. "Who's next then? Come on. I can take you all. How about you, eh?"

The sound of fabric tearing, followed by a frightened yelp.

From inside, a man shouted, "Look out, he's gone berserk!"

Billy dashed through the waiting area and pushed open the door of the treatment room. He saw Doctor Morton standing on a chair, trying to shrink into the wall. Torn papers and the shredded remains of a straw basket lay strewn across the floor. In the far corner, an open cat box lay on its side. A second vet sat beneath the desk with his knees drawn up to his chin, sucking at the back of his hand. The female veterinary assistant peered in through the circular window in the outer door. She looked terrified.

Snowy stood on his hind legs in the middle of the room, shaking a furious paw at everyone. The moment he saw Billy he jumped up at his chest, knocking him backward.

"I thought you'd never come. Please, you have to get me out of here."

"What on earth happened?" Dr. Euston demanded.

The female assistant slid back into the room to help her colleague out from under the desk. Doctor Morton climbed down from the chair, keeping a wary eye on Snowy. "I'm not quite sure. He seemed fine until we tried to put him in the box, then he went crazy."

"He's all right now," Billy said.

Marcus had been hanging back, holding Emma. "Well, no permanent harm done." He surveyed the mess, then handed Emma back to her father. "Perhaps you should take Snowy home now."

They made their way back through the village. Billy carried Snowy, who seemed to have fallen asleep. Emma dozed happily in her father's arms, her head resting against his shoulder.

They hadn't spoken since leaving the research center.

Billy broke the silence. "Dad, please don't tell Mom Snowy scratched everyone. She'd make me give him back to Aggie."

His father considered this for a moment. "He went pretty crazy in there, son. She'd be right to worry."

"But Dad, I told you, Snowy hates cat boxes. He's been as good as gold at home."

"What if he scratched Emma?"

"He wouldn't. She's been trying to ride him since he first came home with us. She's pulled his tail a hundred times, but he's never once scratched her. Please, Dad, Snowy's my only friend apart from Carmen, and she's going back to Paris after the holidays."

His father shifted Emma to his other shoulder. "All right. He can stay. But understand this: If he scratches anyone else, especially your sister, he's out. Is that clear?"

"Absolutely. Thanks, Dad."

"Right. Now let's get home before my arms go completely numb."

His bedroom felt strange, with blank walls and no furniture but his bed. Billy spread bath towels over the floor before giving Snowy his 'welcome home' treat. The smell of cheese-and-onion crispy snacks mingled with the aroma of new carpet as he emptied the packet into a bowl and set it down. "There you are. Your favorite flavor, and for refreshments, a bottle of cola, *with* a bendy straw."

Snowy, who'd finished off a tin of cat food, several

saucers of milk and quite a few of Emma's leftover fries at teatime, tucked in greedily. "I take it you've forgiven me for making a mess the other day."

"Absolutely, I never expected you to throw yourself at the patio door like you did. That was above and beyond the call of duty. I really thought you'd hurt yourself."

"To tell you the truth, I didn't mean to hit the window."

"What?"

"I planned to veer away at the last minute, then hobble around the patio, pretending I'd hurt my leg while you and Carmen went into your *Emergency Ward Ten* routine."

"Why didn't you?"

Snowy stared at the floor and mumbled something.

"Pardon?"

"I said, 'I trod on a frog'. Oi, stop laughing, you."

Billy's entire body shook as a fit of the giggles overcame him. "You mean that spectacular dive, when you ended up splayed out across the glass before sliding down the window, was an accident?"

Snowy bridled. "It's not funny. I hate frogs, Bill. I hate 'em. Whenever I touch one, I spring up in the air. I can't help it."

Billy lay back on his bed with his arms folded across his chest. Tears of laughter rolled down his face into his ears. "Sorry," he gasped. "But you looked so funny with your face pressed up against the window."

The memory of it sent him into fresh convulsions.

"Fat lot of good it did," Snowy grumbled. "Tinhead's family wasn't even there." He took an angry slurp of Cola.

Billy's giggling fit subsided. He sat up and wiped his face. "I know. Sorry about that, but I think I may have found them after all."

"What? Where?"

"I went to *Adventure Safari* yesterday. I saw a vixen and two cubs in the Local Life section. We need to get a description from Razor, but I think it might be them."

"Excellent. We'll have a chat with old Chrome-dome later."

"Would you mind if I stay here?" Billy asked. "My parents are getting suspicious. I don't want to risk getting caught unless it's really important, besides, all these late nights have tired me out."

"That's the trouble with humans," Snowy said. "You've no staying power. Don't worry. I'll give him the good news."

The next morning, Billy awoke to find Snowy standing on his pillow. The cat's whiskers looked unusually droopy. He sat up, rubbing the sleep from his eyes. "Did you see Razor?"

Snowy shook his head, and gestured at the battered, metal helmet by the door. "Billy Euston, we have a problem."

Chapter Ten
Professor Farofas

Razor opened his eyes and stared around him, trying to focus. A bright, unnatural light shone on him from above. Without moving, he took in his surroundings. He lay on a cold, gray, concrete floor, covered with dry sawdust and straw. Brick walls, painted dirty white, hemmed him in on three sides.

The place reeked of disinfectant. He lifted his head. It felt weighed down. He realized someone had put a new helmet on him. Thin straps ran under his chin and upper body to hold it firmly in place. He tried to stand, but his legs turned to jelly.

Behind him, Razor heard the muffled sound of a human voice.

"It takes several minutes after awakening for the subject to regain control of its body. When it has done so, we can begin the demonstration."

Razor rolled onto his other side, panting. A window ran along the length of the far wall, about two feet off the floor. A row of humans stared at him through the glass. In front of them stood a short, weedy little man with a bald head, a bushy beard and cruel eyes.

Fur-Face!

As Razor watched, Fur-Face placed a larger version of the metal helmet on his own head.

"This device simultaneously broadcasts and translates my brainwaves, enabling me to communicate with the subject. Thanks to the tiny microprocessor I implanted in its brain, the animal can now understand me on a subconscious level. Our helmets amplify the signal."

"Can it answer back?" one of the onlookers asked.

Some of the men laughed.

"An excellent question, General Gomez, although I realize you are making with the humorous comment. Eventually, I hope to discover a viable means of making two-way communication possible." Fur-Face gave a little sigh. "However, at present, this is not possible. Unless of course, the animal broadcasts to a human naturally attuned to receiving its signals." He shook his head and chuckled as another man raised a hand. "I'm afraid the odds of that happening are many billion to one. I was merely making with the funny joke."

Fur-Face brought his hands together with a loud 'smack'. "Let us begin the demonstration."

Razor staggered to his feet, his legs still shaky. The humans stared at him through the window. He could understand them all, but when Fur-Face spoke, it sounded like the professor had somehow climbed inside his head. Right now, he wanted him to walk to the other wall.

Razor snarled. "Go bite yourself, human."

"There seems to be a lack of cooperation from your pet fox," Gomez sneered.

"My dear General, all he needs is a little persuasion." Fur-Face pressed a button on the small box in his hand.

White hot pain lanced through Razor's head. With a tortured howl, he sprang backward, clawing at the metal helmet, but it wouldn't come off. A few seconds later, the pain receded. He opened his eyes to find himself lying, exhausted, at the back of his cell.

On the other side of the window Fur-Face gave him a cold smile, then turned back to address the others. "I sent a pain message directly to the subject's nervous system. Once the animal understands non-compliance equals agonizing pain, it will cooperate. I have had many successes with smaller subjects, although some allowed themselves to be driven insane before giving in. Let us try again."

Fur-Face pressed a different button on the box. His voice echoed in Razor's head.

"COME TO THE WINDOW."

To the obvious surprise of the spectators, Razor struggled to his feet and staggered across the floor.

After ten minutes of obediently moving from one part of his cell to another, he flopped down in a heap as, outside in the viewing room, Fur-Face removed his helmet and invited questions.

General Gomez, who seemed to be the leader of the group, looked skeptical. "It's all very well to make it move around a room, but what use is that to us?"

"Well," Fur-Face said. "I suppose we could tell farmers to pay us money, or we send foxes in to eat their chickens, ha-ha-ha-ha."

The joke was met with a stony silence.

Fur-Face threw open his arms. "Gentlemen, can you not see the possibilities? Can you not imagine the incredible opportunities this technology opens up for

125

you?"

"I'm a soldier," Gomez snapped. "I'm not paid to have an imagination. Why don't you do it for me?"

"Very well," Fur-Face said. "What if we fitted a dog with an internal explosive device? Using my invention, you could send it to your target from a safe distance." He gestured through the window at Razor. "This very animal escaped during trials. I used the opportunity to test the homing signal I built into the brain chip. I've sent dozens of my programmed rats to find the source. Two of them from over five miles away. They all reached the target."

Next to the general, a man in a dark suit asked,-"The theory seems fine, Professor, but how soon will you be able to amplify the signals you send without the, er...subject...having to wear a metal receiver?"

"With the proper funding and facilities, I can complete the project in a little over two years. Now, unless there are any further questions, I believe we have concluded our demonstration. The auction will take place over the internet, one week from today. Bidding starts at two-hundred-and-fifty-million American dollars. There can be only one successful buyer."

"Hold on a minute," General Gomez said. "Why did you use a fox here? What success have you had with other animals? For a quarter of a billion dollars, I'll need a little more convincing."

Fur-Face turned on him. "I have already explained. I brought you here to see the potential. As for the money, how much would you pay to be able to remove all those troublesome individuals, too closely guarded for you to reach? In the future, you may even be able to use the technology for spying. After all, even the President of your United States has a dog, does he not?"

Razor listened, but most of what he heard made no sense. When the humans left, he lay down in the corner and tried to sleep. Nothing to do now but wait, and hope for a chance to escape.

Somehow, he didn't think it would be as easy as the last time.

Billy sat on the couch with his head in his hands. "It's my fault. If I'd gone out to see him the other night, this would never have happened."

Snowy jumped up beside him. "Cheer up. We can't be sure they got him."

"Oh yes we can. You know he'd never willingly leave his helmet behind. I really thought we'd found his family. Now I don't know what to do."

"Maybe it's time we got some help."

"Who from? My parents already think I'm losing my mind."

"I suppose you're right," Snowy said. "Besides, we need to be careful. Human brains alter as they grow older. They can't cope with things not doing what they're supposed to. Whatever proof we give them, they'd convince themselves it was a coincidence, or a hallucination."

Billy picked up Razor's helmet. "You've got a point. I didn't want to believe it myself at first, and I'm only thirteen."

"Even if we could prove it, I'd spend the rest of my life in some science lab being poked around by a bunch of boring academic types like your friend Marcus. I don't fancy that much."

They sat in gloomy silence for a while, then Snowy said. "What about Carmen? She knows about computers. Maybe she could trace old Tin-head from Aggie's house."

"I don't know. Besides, how do we prove you can talk? Only I can hear you."

"You just get her here, leave the rest to me."

That afternoon, Carmen cycled to Billy's house. "I'm glad you called," she said, when Billy opened the front door. "I made something for you."

She watched a broad smile spread across his face as he pulled a dark blue T-shirt from the plastic bag she offered him and held it up. "Aggie suggested it. I scanned the drawing of Static-Man I did for you the other day, then printed it on one of those iron-on T-shirt transfers."

He beamed at her. "I don't know what to say. This is awesome." He suddenly turned to look at Snowy, who sat at the top of the stairs. "Right." He nodded, then said, "Listen, I can't thank you enough, but right now, I need to show you something."

A few minutes later, Carmen sat on Billy's new carpet, with her back resting against the side of his bed. She held up a playing card. "Ready."

From downstairs by the front door, Billy called out, "Four of diamonds."

"Amazing. How did you do it?" She held the card up to the window and turned it back to front. No light came through. All she could see was the blue squiggly pattern on the back.

"Try another," Billy said.

He'd started by having her select a random card from the pack. She'd held it in front of her face, keeping it hidden, but Billy had correctly guessed which one. He'd repeated the trick, moving farther away each time.

She grinned to herself, then placed the deck of cards, face down, on the floor. "Ready when you are."

"No you're not, you didn't pick a card."

Carmen's jaw dropped, then she smiled. "Wait, I know. You've got a camera somewhere, right?"

Billy came back upstairs, wearing his new T-shirt. "Not exactly." He nodded at Snowy, who'd been sitting on the bed the whole time. "I had a little help."

She stared at the cat.

"No, seriously, how did you do it? Have you hidden a camera somewhere?"

They argued for some time. In the end, he sat her on the bed. "I'm telling you the truth. Snowy can speak, but only I can hear him. I don't know what else I can do to prove it."

She went to the window. Out in the back yard, Emma and Mrs. Euston planted seeds in one of the flowerbeds. "I believe you *think* he can talk Billy, but there has to be a more logical explanation."

"Please, Carmen, don't use your brain, just trust me. We did the card thing. You opened books at random and Snowy told me the page number. We even played Monopoly for a bit. How many cats can do that?"

Snowy had curled up on Billy's computer chair, but sat up at the word 'Monopoly'.

"He just said he wants to be the car next time." Billy

gave Carmen an imploring look. "If I wanted to trick you, I'd make up something better than that, wouldn't I?"

"This is all too weird. I think I'd better be going."

"Wait. he's telling me something else."

He really did seem to be listening to the cat, although Snowy made no sound. Poor kid, she thought, the strain of moving away from London must have got to him.

Billy's earnest expression changed to something between surprise and shock. "Snowy saw you when you arrived at Aggie's on Friday. He says she brought you back from the station in the Land Rover."

Carmen headed for the door. "She'd hardly collect me on the bike, I had suitcases with me."

"He says you talked about missing someone."

"Oh, give it up, Bill. I've already told you I miss my mom. I'm leaving now. Goodbye."

She made if halfway down the stairs before he called out again.

"Not your mother. You said, Jean-Pierre. You said you missed Jean-Pierre."

Carmen stopped in her tracks. "What did you say?"

Billy leaned over the banister rail. "Snowy followed you into the house. You left your cases in the hall, then went into the kitchen. Aggie gave him some milk, with no bloomin' straw." He paused to give the cat an exasperated look. "At the kitchen table, you told Aggie about Jean-Pierre. You showed her the picture you keep in your locket."

She pulled a silver chain from around her neck. "How could you know?"

"Because Snowy knows, and he told me. You told

Aggie you hope to marry him one day."

She felt the color drain from her face. In a daze, she walked back upstairs. "This is incredible. That cat can talk."

Billy spread towels over his new carpet, then fetched some snacks from the kitchen.

"Carmen, before we go on. You have to promise not to tell anyone about this. I don't want Snowy ending up in some science lab."

"I won't tell. Who'd believe me anyway?" She stared at Snowy, who had his head buried inside a packet of crispy snacks. "I can hardly believe it myself. It must have been really weird when you found yourself talking to a dumb animal."

"I admit, it felt a bit odd at first, but he's actually quite smart, in his own limited way."

Billy let out a deep sigh, then leaned forward to brush some crumbs from the cat's back. "Snowy, she was talking to *me*."

"Pardon?" Carmen asked.

"Nothing," Billy said. "We need your help."

He told her everything. When he'd finished she said, "Of course, now I see why you got so excited about the Local Life section, but what is it you think I can do?"

"We want you to get into the computer system at the research center. With any luck, you might find a clue to where Farofas took Razor."

"Didn't Aggie say she had him kicked off the project?"

"Yes, but Razor told me Fur-Face has an assistant called Gallstone. That sounds too much like Gladstone to be a coincidence. I think this 'Fur-Face' is Doctor Farofas. He only took Razor last month, so he must have set up a new laboratory, somewhere nearby."

Carmen sat back in Billy's chair. "You've been watching too many spy movies. This is Little Chumberry not Hollywood. You can't just switch on someone else's computer and instantly find what you're looking for. There'd be passwords"

"But aren't you some kind of computer wizard."

"I can use a computer, yes, but I couldn't hack into one if my life depended on it."

Snowy held up a paw. "Excuse me."

"Besides," Carmen added, "I don't want to poke around in Aggie's computer system without her permission. It wouldn't be right."

Snowy tried again. "Hello, I have a suggestion."

Billy still ignored him. "Surely, the passwords would be something simple, like your name, or a favorite animal." His face brightened. "I bet it's Mr. Tinkles."

"I don't care. I won't do it."

A high-pitched, scratching noise brought the argument to a sudden halt.

Snowy continued to scrape his front claws along the radiator until he had their undivided attention. "I know I'm only a dumb animal, but I can't understand why you always have to do things the hard way."

"What do you mean?"

"I mean," Snowy gestured at Carmen, "I never said Carmen should hack into anyone's computer."

"Well, how are we supposed to get at the information?" Billy said. "Aggie's not going to just type in the passwords and leave us to it, is she?"

Carmen couldn't have known what Snowy had said, but she heard Billy's reply. "Actually, I think she might, if I asked her. Aggie's really proud of what she's set up at *Adventure Safari*. I bet she'd be delighted we took such an interest."

"Thank you," Snowy said. "It's good to know at least one of you can use a brain. If I were you, Bill, I'd steam in there and marry that girl. She's wasted on that French kid."

"He talked then, didn't he?" Carmen said. "What did he say?"

Billy's cheeks burned red. "He said 'Well done.' How soon can you get a look at everything?"

"I'll ask her tonight, but you need to tell me what I'm searching for."

Billy wandered around his room, making suggestions, while Carmen sat at his desk and wrote a list of things to search for. "We need to check there isn't really someone called Gallstone on the payroll."

"Gallstone…payroll…"

Billy stopped walking around. "Good idea, Snowy. He says we should check the building plans, in case they built another research site, somewhere near *Adventure Safari*."

Carmen scribbled on the page. "That looks so weird when he talks to you. Farofas would need a bit of space to work in. While I'm at it, I should check if they built any animal holding areas away from the main site."

They spent another few minutes trying to think of things to add to the list, but no one came up with anything, so Carmen got ready to go home.

"You sure you want to do this?" Billy asked.

A fierce look appeared on her face. "Someone's using Aggie's park and the research center as a cover for something bad. I won't let anyone hurt my grandmother's reputation. Call me if you think of anything else."

At the front gate Billy stood with Snowy, watching Carmen cycle off through the village.

"Yep," Snowy muttered. "You should definitely marry her."

He didn't answer. For some reason he'd felt a sharp pain in his stomach when Snowy first mentioned Jean-Pierre. He knew nothing about the boy, except he didn't like him.

"Come on, let's get inside."

Chapter Eleven
Finding Scala

Razor lay in his cell, shivering. Cold and miserable, he hadn't eaten since before his capture. His thoughts turned to Scala and the cubs. A wave of despair swept over him.

Why doesn't he just kill me and get it over with?

He threw back his head and howled.

Gladstone hurried in from the next room, followed by Fur-Face, who barged past his assistant to grab the remote control from the window ledge. "Be quiet, you stupid animal!"

For the second time that day, white-hot pain lanced through Razor's head. This time, it felt like his brain boiled inside his head. He blacked out. When he came to, he found himself lying on his side, too exhausted to even roll over.

From the other room, human voices filtered through the pain into his conscious mind.

"You fool, if you killed him–"

"How dare you talk to me like that?"

Then someone else spoke.

"He dares because I pay him to."

The voice sounded deep and powerful. Razor had never heard it before, but he instinctively knew its owner was used to being obeyed.

The newcomer's footsteps crossed the outer room. "You look surprised, Doctor Farofas. Perhaps you expected someone else?"

"No, sir, of course not."

Razor opened his eyes. From where he lay, the fluorescent light in his cell reflected off the window pane, making it hard to see what happened on the other side.

The safety glass rattled as Fur-Face's body slammed against the window, his white coat flattened out across the glass. "Do you take me for some kind of imbecile? General Gomez will not be joining you today, or any other day for that matter."

Fur-Face had been lifted quite a way up the window now, his legs flailed about as he struggled to break free. "You can't kill me. Only I can make this work. Without me you have nothing."

"True, we wouldn't have got this far without you, Doctor. You opened the door and showed us the way."

Fur-Face made desperate choking sounds. Razor could smell the man's terror.

"But once a door's been opened," the voice continued, "others can easily walk on through. Isn't that right, Doctor Gladstone?"

"Actually, sir," Gladstone said. "He keeps the most important details in his head. It would take several years to acquire that knowledge, should his services be lost to us."

"Really? You're a lucky man, Farofas. People who cross me, rarely live long enough to regret it. I wouldn't waste the opportunity if I were you."

Farofas dropped to the floor like a dead stoat.

The newcomer leaned over him. "Have I made myself absolutely clear?"

"Yes, sir." Fur-Face gasped.

"Now then, gentlemen." The voice lost some of its menacing tone. "As I understand it, this fox is the only decent subject we've got. So why does he look half-starved?"

Gladstone spoke from the darkness. "I will see to it this instant."

"You'd better. The Russian delegation arrives in less than forty-eight hours. I've decided to spice up the display with a little 'David & Goliath' show afterward. I want this fox looking a lot healthier by Sunday afternoon, and I want the adjoining cell ready for a new guest by this evening. I don't need to tell you how disappointed I'll be if things don't go well. Goodnight…gentlemen."

As the stranger's footsteps receded, the tension in the air lifted. Without a word to each other, Gladstone and Farofas left the outer room.

A short while later, a small hatch at the bottom of the cell door slid open. Someone pushed a bowl of water through the gap, followed by a plate, piled high with chunks of raw meat.

Razor guzzled down the food first, then took a long drink. Afterward, he curled up in a lonely ball in the corner of his cell and tried to get some sleep.

Carmen cycled back from Billy's house in a daze, still reeling from the discovery that Snowy could talk. At the open gateway in front of Aggie's mansion, she took off her fluorescent pink safety helmet and walked her bike to the house. Engrossed in her thoughts, she crunched up the gravel driveway, not registering the strange car parked next to her grandmother's Land Rover until she had almost reached it.

She'd never seen a stretched limousine this big. Apart from the black tires and dark, one-way glass in the windows, the entire car seemed to be made out of polished gold. Carmen looked for number plates, but found none. Curious to learn more about Aggie's wealthy visitor, she took her bike to the side of the house and hurried around to the front door.

As she stepped into the hall, she heard laughter coming from the drawing room. It grew suddenly louder as the door opened and Helen came out, carrying a tray of empty glasses.

"Hello, Carmen. You'd better go straight through. We have a visitor." She hurried into the kitchen, still giggling.

Aggie called out from the drawing room. "Carmen, dear, is that you? Come on in. I want you to meet an old friend of mine."

When Carmen entered she saw a great, silver-haired bear of a man. Well over six feet tall and built like one of those implausibly large wrestlers she'd seen on television. His body looked ready to explode out of the tailor-made dinner suit he wore. He'd been leaning on the wall by the fireplace, facing Aggie, but when he saw her, his rugged, good-natured face, split into a wide grin.

The broad, Texan accent was unmistakable. "Howdy, little princess, Benedict Barnum at your service, and with those beautiful brown eyes, you just *have* to be Aggie's granddaughter."

Carmen didn't quite know what to say. "Yes... Pleased to meet you, Mr. Barnum." She took his outstretched hand, half-expecting him to crush her fingers within his giant paw.

His gentle grip surprised her. "Please, call me Benny, all my friends do." As he leaned in closer, the smell of his sandalwood cologne wafted over her. "Maybe you can help me, Carmen. We open the new Sea View section at *Adventure Safari* on Sunday. I've asked Aggie to conduct the opening ceremony on my behalf." Barnum stepped back to the fireplace. "She knows I'll just stand there and make a damn fool of myself, but the stubborn woman refuses to help me out."

Aggie laughed. "Benedict Barnum, you know perfectly well you have to open it. People want to see the man who funded the park and research center." She grinned at Carmen. "Benny and I have been friends since we were your age. His father was the American Ambassador in Hong Kong. We studied Chinese boxing together."

"We sure did," Barnum chuckled. "And I don't mind telling you, this sweet little lady kicked my oversized butt around the yard more times than I care to remember."

Helen came in with a tray of drinks and announced their dinner would be ready in twenty minutes, then gave Carmen's jeans and T-shirt a meaningful look.

She took the hint and changed into the turquoise dress her mother had insisted she bring to England, 'Just in case you need to look smart.' She decided to wait until later before asking about the blueprints for the park.

At Aggie's insistence, Helen joined them for dinner.

They enjoyed a wonderful meal. Barnum and Aggie spent the whole time reminiscing. Carmen found herself swept along with their infectious laughter as the two old friends came up with story after story, each one funnier than the last.

Despite wanting to talk to Aggie alone, she felt disappointed when Barnum refused an after dinner coffee, and set off for a late meeting he had scheduled in town.

"You two seemed very cozy," she said, as they helped Helen clear the table. "In fact, the way you flirted with each other, I wouldn't be surprised if you two didn't get engaged soon."

Aggie put the last of the dishes on a tray. "He already asked me once, years ago. I can't say I wasn't tempted. Benny's been a good friend, but I'm not sure I'd prefer him as a husband." She took Carmen's arm and they went through into the sitting room. "Besides, no one could take the place of your grandfather. Now, what is it you've been itching to ask me since you came back from Billy's house?"

"Was I so obvious, Grandma?"

"Only to a seasoned professional like me. Your father used to get the same look about him when he had something exciting to pass on and didn't want to wait."

"It's nothing exciting really." She wanted to tell her all about Snowy, but she'd made a promise. "Billy wants to design his own theme park. I said I'd ask if I could borrow a copy of the blueprints for *Adventure Safari*, to give him some ideas."

"Is that all," Aggie laughed. "I half expected to hear you two had become an item."

"Oh very funny. I like Billy, but he's just a friend."

"All right, dear, I'm only pulling your leg. Come with me to the office, we can dig out those blueprints before we go to bed."

The next morning, Billy carried Carmen's backpack to his room. It was overflowing with drawings, engineering reports and maps of the old copper mine.

Once it became clear there'd be no space for food amongst all the documents on the bedroom floor, Snowy left them to it.

The two friends stood on the bed, staring at the maze of paperwork on the carpet. "Maybe we should just use the blueprints for *Adventure Safari*'s tunnel structure."

When they'd finished, they had a semi-accurate layout of the park's underground spread over the floor.

"Now what?" Carmen asked.

Billy picked his way to the desk and held up a brochure. "This is a Visitor Guide. I kept it from the other day. We need to match up the tunnels with the topside areas. We know the main reptile section is directly above the underground dome, so let's start there."

They covered the tunnel layout with colored sheets from Billy's scrap pad. When every area had been accounted for, they stood on the bed again to survey the results.

"Nothing," Carmen said. "I felt sure we'd find an unexplained bit of tunnel somewhere."

Billy went to the door to get a different view. "Maybe we just need to look at it differently. Let's think this through. If you wanted to set up an unauthorized research laboratory beneath the park, where would you put it?"

"I don't know. How much room would I need?"

"Well, you'd need space for all your equipment, at least twice the size of this room."

Carmen sat the desk, making notes. "You'd need more than that. You'd have animals to keep. Hold on, the other day, Aggie said they'd wanted to open part of the underground section to the public, but there were too many security concerns. I wonder if they got as far as doing the digging for it before they changed their minds."

Billy picked up the colored sheets to reveal the underground layout.

While she waited, Carmen rolled out the original tunnel blueprints on the desk. "According to these, they dug up a large area about where you're standing now. That would be more or less beneath the tigers, wouldn't it?"

"I think so. Can you tell if they finished building it?"

"They're bound to have left notes." Carmen grabbed a fistful of documents. She passed some to Billy. "You never know, we might get lucky."

A few minutes later, Billy unfolded a plan for the underground electrical system. "How about this?"

She studied the plan over his shoulder. "Look, those cables routed into the storage section. I bet when we line this up with the tunnel blueprints, we'll find your unauthorized lab."

"Perhaps," Billy said. "It's well away from the rest

of the system, but still, you'd think someone would have noticed it."

"I don't suppose anyone goes out that far." Carmen ran her finger along the blueprint. "See, it's a good half-mile from the central dome."

"What is?"

Snowy stood in the doorway, surveying the room. "I hope your mom doesn't see this mess."

They tidied everything away, then told Snowy about their suspicions.

"Good work," Snowy said. "So, what do we do now?"

"I think we need to find out if the vixen we saw really is Scala. She might be able to tell us more about Fur-Face's lab."

Snowy jumped on the window ledge. "How'd you plan to manage that? Unless she's wearing one of Tin-head's helmets, you won't be able to speak to her."

"True," Billy grinned. "But you can."

It didn't take long to persuade Billy's mother that a Saturday afternoon at *Adventure Safari* was just what the family needed. Dr. Euston didn't seem quite as keen, he saw it every day at work, but allowed himself to be persuaded. There was, however, a big argument with Snowy, who became quite upset when Billy informed him he'd only be allowed in the park if he wore a collar and lead.

"Do I *look* like a bloody dog?" he said, and stomped off.

Billy followed him into the back yard while everyone else stood by the car, chatting to Aggie.

143

"Come on, you know I can't do this without you."

Snowy frowned at him from the shed roof. "I haven't worn a collar since that psychopath threw me off the bridge. I don't intend to start now."

"That's not fair and you know it. I'd never let anyone hurt you. Besides, Razor saved your life once. You owe him."

Snowy thought about it, then jumped onto the water barrel. "It must be those rotten human urges. I never had a conscience before." He sat upright and stretched out his neck. "Go on, but if I hear any dog walking jokes, someone's gonna get their trousers shredded."

When they reached *Adventure Safari*, Billy felt a twinge of disappointment as his father joined the line of visitors' cars instead of heading for the staff entrance. Wary of being trodden on, Snowy insisted on being carried until they got through the turnstiles.

It had rained earlier, but the bright sunshine promised a warm afternoon.

Snowy sniffed the air. "Let me see…hot dogs, popcorn and something else." He seemed puzzled for a moment, then grinned. "Oh yes, elephant poop." He rubbed himself against Billy's legs. "I'm starving, where's the food area? No, scratch that. First I need to take a leak. I knew I shouldn't have had a second cola. Walk me to the nearest rubbish bin would you?"

As Billy led him to the garbage can on the other side of the path, he heard his father tell Carmen, "Primal instinct, you know. It's in their genes. Snowy only just got here, but he's already marking it as his own territory."

Snowy grinned at Billy from behind the bin. "Your

dad knows his stuff, doesn't he?"

The Open-top Tram Ride took them on a leisurely tour around the park. When they passed the new Sea View area, they saw laborers, dressed in blue overalls and bright yellow hard hats, setting up a platform in front of the entrance for the next day's grand opening.

At the end of the ride, Billy gave in to Snowy's incessant nagging, and suggested they get something to eat. They went to the dining area outside the entrance to the Reptile House of Horrors, where a group of Japanese tourists had just vacated one of the dark brown plastic tables.

Dr. Euston took the food requests.

"I'll have a crocodile sandwich," Snowy said, "and make it snappy, hehehe."

Billy burst out laughing.

His father gave him a curious look.

"Sorry, Dad. A hotdog and fries for me, please. Want some help?"

He joined the food queue with his father. Along with the crocodile sandwich, Snowy's request for toad-in-the-hole also went unheeded, so he made do with some of Emma's fries.

Afterward, Mrs. Euston agreed to let Carmen and Billy wander off on their own. "Meet us by the Giraffe Slide at four o'clock," she said, as they headed toward the tiger enclosure with Snowy. "And don't be late."

"That gives us a little over an hour," Carmen said, as they set off. "We've got plenty of time."

They strolled down the path toward the Local Life section, with Snowy trotting along between them like a feline chaperone. On the way, they stopped to look at a field of gophers.

Carmen leaned against the wooden railings which separated the main path from the enclosure. "I wonder why you can hear Snowy but I can't?"

Billy pulled a face, having spent the last few minutes trying to ignore his cat's rather tuneless impression of Elvis Presley. "I don't know, but at the moment I wish I couldn't. He's just murdered one of my dad's favorite songs."

Snowy stopped in mid-verse. "Kids today have no appreciation for the classics."

Billy repeated the comment.

"It isn't fair," Carmen moaned. "I've been coming here every year since I can remember, but nothing exciting ever happened to me. You turn up and on your very first day you meet a talking cat. I'm very jealous."

Snowy chuckled. "Not half as jealous as he is of Jean-Pierre."

"Shut up, Snowy." The horrible, gnawing sensation in Billy's stomach returned. He leaned against the fence beside Carmen, fixing his gaze on one of the gophers. It stood on its hind legs, motionless and alert. "I'm not really the adventurous type," he muttered. "I don't feel comfortable with all this secret stuff."

She nudged his arm. "Liar."

He opened his mouth to speak, but her smile distracted him. He looked away, confused.

"Ahem. Hello!" Snowy stood on his hind legs to paw at Billy's knee. "We came here to check on Razor's missus, remember?"

"Right." Billy stepped away from the rail. "We'd best get going."

It didn't take long to reach the fox compound. Billy spotted the vixen straight away, curled up beside her cubs on the roof of their hut. They looked asleep.

"What now?" Carmen asked.

"We need to get their attention." They both looked at Snowy.

"Forget it, I'm not going in there. They'd rip me to shreds."

"You don't have to," Billy said. "Just call her over."

Snowy jumped on the notice board in front of the fence. After a quick look around to make sure they were alone, he scratched at the wooden panel.

The vixen looked at them.

Snowy waved his front legs in the air. "Kissie-kissie-kissie. Here, vixie-vixie. Here, vixie-vixie." He giggled, then put his paw to his mouth. "Oi-oi, oi-oi, oi-oi, oi."

"What's he doing?" Carmen asked.

"Trying to be funny. All right, very amusing, now pack it in and talk to her properly."

"Yes, your bleeding highness," Snowy sat up straight. "Oi, missus, you don't happen to know old Tin-head would you?" He saw Billy's scowl. "I mean, excuse me, madam, my friends and I thought you might be acquainted with a friend of ours? A fox named Razor. In fact, we're rather hoping you and those delightful-looking cubs might be his missing family." He looked at Billy. "Better?"

"Very nice. Now behave yourself, she's coming over."

At the sound of Razor's name, the vixen jumped from the roof. She trotted to the fence, leaving the two sleeping cubs behind her. She cocked her head to one side, then Snowy said, "Hold on love. I need to translate for the human."

While they talked, Carmen studied the two animals. Whenever Snowy spoke to Billy, the cat's face took on a slightly unnatural expression, but when he talked to the vixen, he looked more like he was sniffing at the air for something.

The conversation went slowly, because Snowy had to translate everything for Billy and Scala, but eventually, the vixen trotted off to rejoin her cubs.

"So, what did we find out?" she asked, as they headed back up the path.

"Scala says she woke up here, the day after the humans attacked. She doesn't know where Razor could be, but the tunnels must run right under the enclosure. Last night she thought she heard a fox screaming, somewhere in the ground beneath their hut."

At the Jungle Trek area, they saw Emma climbing the steps of the Giraffe Slide with her mother. Dr. Euston stood on his own, leaning against the safety fence on the other side of the path, absentmindedly licking at an ice cream cone. He seemed pre-occupied with something.

"Hi, Dad, what's up?" Billy asked.

"Not sure. We got here a few minutes ago. I thought I'd check in on one of my patients while your mother took Emma for another go on the slide."

"Mr. Tinkles is missing," Carmen said.

"How could you possibly know about Mr. Tinkles?" She did her best to keep a straight face.

"Elementary, my dear Dr. Euston. The gorillas live here in the Jungle Trek area. The other day, Marcus said he'd been sent back here. As far as I know, there've been no other operations. You look concerned, so there must have been some kind of problem. If Mr. Tinkles was in there, but ill, you'd have stayed to sort it out. Therefore, the only other possibility is that he's not here. A straightforward deduction really."

Billy's jaw dropped. "Amazing."

While Carmen had been talking, Snowy jumped on the wooden railing where he leaned over to lick, unnoticed, at Dr. Euston's ice cream. "Also," she continued, "Benedict Barnum, the man who funds the research center, came to Aggie's for dinner last night. I heard them talking about sending Mr. Tinkles to his zoo in Ohio, which may also have helped."

They all laughed.

Mrs. Euston appeared, carrying a very tired-looking Emma in her arms.

As they made their way through the car park, Snowy pulled on his lead.

"Hang on a sec," Billy said. "I think he needs to mark his territory again before we go." He leaned in to Carmen and whispered, "He says my Dad's ice cream was cold."

Chapter Twelve
Mission Implausible

Back at home, Billy took his fellow conspirators to his room. "The way I see it, if Farofas really has a lab beneath the park, it's directly under the Local Life section. Scala said she'd heard other noises from what she called 'the big holes' beneath her enclosure."

Carmen sat at Billy's desk, poring over the main blueprint for the tunnel system. "It doesn't make sense. According to the layout we made, there shouldn't be anything there at all."

"I know, but our map was pretty basic. We thought the unused display area lay under the tiger pens, which are pretty close to where Scala is."

"So what now?"

Snowy curled up on the bed. "How about dinner?"

Billy ignored him. "We need to get into those tunnels to find Razor, then we need to tell Aggie what's been going on. She'll know what to do."

"We can show her these blueprints," Carmen said. "Maybe suggest it as a convalescing area for animals, like the one they've got at the research center." She gestured at Snowy, who'd jumped off the bed to push Billy toward the door with his front paws. "What's the matter with him?"

"He wants something to eat."

"Again?"

"I know. Stop it, Snowy, we need to decide our next move."

Snowy kept pushing. "What next move? We found Tin-head's missus, just like he wanted. It's not our fault he got himself caught."

"Razor saved your life," Billy said. "Why are you being so selfish?"

"I'm a cat, it's in our makeup. Anyway, who are you to call me selfish?"

"What's that supposed to mean?"

"It means I'm not the only one around here with his own best interests at heart. You think Razor protected me from that other fox out of kindness? If he hadn't needed me to find a human, he'd have happily watched me get eaten. Hell, he'd have killed me himself, just for the fun of it. Foxes are vicious, spiteful beggars when they want to be."

"He still saved your life."

"And what about you?" Snowy's tail twitched with agitation. "I heard you and your dad on the way back from the vetstipal." He mimicked Billy's voice. '*Please, Dad, Snowy's my only friend apart from Carmen, and she's going back to Paris after the holidays*'. If you could find a few mates your own age around here, I wouldn't get a look in, and nor would Razor for that matter. From where I'm sitting, pal, that makes you just as selfish as me. The only difference is, I'm honest enough to admit it."

Billy opened his mouth to reply, but realized Snowy had a point. He sat on the bed. "Carmen, I know this seems weird, but could you give us a minute?"

151

"Sure, I'll get us something to eat."

Billy lay on his bed, with his hands behind his head.

Snowy sat beside him. "Sorry. I shouldn't have said all those things."

Billy scratched the top of the cat's head. "I'm not good at making friends." He closed his eyes. "Back in London, most of the other kids avoided me, except for Patrick. Whenever he wasn't at school, I just wandered around the playground on my own."

He pulled Carmen's Static-Man drawing off the wall, tracing the superhero's yellow and red costume with his finger. "That's why I made up this fellow. Whenever I feel lonely, I work on a story about him and Electric Bill. Pretty dumb, huh?"

Snowy said nothing.

Billy took the picture to his desk. "When I first heard about moving here, away from where I'd lived all my life, I was terrified." He pulled a thick folder from the shelf. "These are all the drawings I've worked on since then. I did fifteen pages on my first afternoon here." He let the folder thump onto the desk. "But you know what? I haven't made up a single story since the day we met, even though Carmen has been giving me drawing lessons."

Snowy cocked his head to one side. "I don't understand."

"I mean, I don't feel lonely any more. I've got you. It wouldn't matter if a hundred kids my age lived in the village, you'd still be my friend. I shouldn't be trying to make you do something you don't want to do. I got carried away with this whole adventure. Nothing exciting ever happened to me before. I wasn't thinking about what you wanted. Sorry."

Carmen came back upstairs with a trayload of drinks and snacks. "Okay, so what have we decided?" She saw the expression on Billy's face. "We can't just give up. What about Aggie? Look, I don't pretend to understand why this Farofas character wants your fox friend, but whatever he's been doing is bound to come out sooner or later. When it does, Aggie will get blamed because the park belongs to her."

"Sorry, Carmen. I don't know what else to do."

Snowy jumped up. "For starters, we can sort out how to get me inside those tunnels so I can find Razor. Come on, Bill, let's have another look at those blueprints. Between the three of us, we can figure it out."

"You mean it?" Billy said. "Really?"

"I mean it." Snowy sniffed at the tray in Carmen's hands. "But first, how about we tuck into some of this grub? It might help jumpstart a few of those 'little gray cells'."

That night, after his parents had gone to sleep, Snowy stood on the kitchen table so Billy could fasten a black lunch bag onto his back. "I hope nobody sees me like this," he muttered. "I feel like a right berk."

Billy checked off his list. "Mini torch, map, crispy snacks, everything's here. Are you sure you don't need any camouflage, for when you get inside *Adventure Safari*? Aggie said they've got security cameras all over the place."

"Bill, it's the middle of the night, I'm a black cat, wearing a pair of sunglasses. How much more camouflaged could I get?"

"Good point, sorry." Billy helped him put on the backpack. "Come on, I'll walk you to the shed."

"What if your dad catches you?"

"I'll risk it."

They slipped out into the back yard. Clouds blocked out the moonlight, and by the time they'd reached the shed, Billy could hardly see Snowy. He crouched in front of the small dark shape at his feet. "You sure you want to do this?"

Snowy's voice came back at him from the shed roof. "Why are you talking to Emma's horse-on-wheels?"

"My shoelace came undone," Billy lied. "You know what you have to do?"

"I'll try not to be insulted by your lack of faith. Wish me luck."

Snowy turned and melted into the darkness.

Billy stared after him. "Good luck," he whispered, "and be careful."

After a while, he walked back toward the house. Halfway up the path, a sudden rustling in the bushes startled him. He whirled around, squinting into the darkness.

Snowy stepped onto the lawn. "It's only me," he said. "*Adventure Safari*'s this way."

Not long after he entered the wood, Snowy tripped over yet another tree root. "Stupid sunglasses." He thought about taking them off, but he had no more room in his backpack and the light reflecting off his eyes would make him easy to spot once he reached the park. He hurried on, lifting his paws a little higher than normal.

About an hour later, he emerged from the trees on the far side of the wood and crossed a field to the hedgerow which marked the boundary of *Adventure Safari*. He scrambled through, then stopped to get his bearings. "According to my calculations," he muttered, "this should be the mongoose enclosure." He peered through the metal bars at a huge mound of dung beside the fence. "Which means they're either a heck of a lot bigger than they look on the visitor map, or I'm in the wrong place."

He stared at the metal barrel on top of the tall, metal railings. Why would someone put that there?

Just then, a female elephant sauntered over. The barrel rattled as she turned it around with her trunk. Dozens of peanuts fell from a hole inside to land in the dirt below.

Not wanting to startle her, Snowy cleared his throat before speaking. "Ahem, excuse me, love, can I have a word?"

The elephant looked bored.

"Don't worry, I'm not a cat burglar." He waited for a laugh, but it didn't come. "Er, which way to the Reptile House, love?"

The elephant considered the question for a moment, then pointed with her trunk to the far side of the enclosure.

"Thanks." He slipped through the metal bars. "Like I said, just passing through."

With the elephant following close behind, Snowy trotted across the enclosure, then through the railings on the far side. "Thanks, Mrs. Jumbo. Listen, if you ever have problems with mice, give me a shout. I'll sort 'em out for you."

The elephant rewarded him with a blank stare.

Strange odors from the various animal enclosures confused his sense of smell, making it hard to get his bearings, but he eventually found himself standing beside the table outside the Reptile House, where the Eustons had eaten, the previous afternoon.

So far so good.

Billy had said he could get into the Underground Waste Disposal system through the large bin behind the Reptile House.

Confident now, he made his way along the wall to the far corner of the building and peeked around the corner. With a horrified yowl, he jerked his head back and stood on his hind legs, his spine pressed against the brickwork as a wave of fear and nausea swept over him.

"Frogs." He forced himself to take a deep breath. "Why did it have to be frogs?"

It took a while to regain his composure, but in the end he steeled his nerves and forced himself to walk around the corner. There were five frogs in all. The four smaller ones stood on the grass, near the dining tables. He focused on them first, then, once his heart rate had slowed to only twice its normal rate, he turned his attention to the largest. It loomed out of the darkness by the edge of the path. At least three feet tall, its huge, bulging eyes stared right back at him. The creature's mouth stood wide open in an obscene grin. Snowy knew he would easily fit inside. He suppressed a shudder.

It took a full minute to summon his courage. *This better work.* He sprinted forward. When he got within a few feet of the giant frog, he launched himself into its gaping jaws.

A few moments later, he picked himself off the hard floor, sniffing the air with distaste. "This place could do with some potpourri."

He dug the torch out from his backpack. As Billy had predicted, he found himself inside the wide metal pipe which transported garbage to the underground waste disposal room. He pointed the torch upward. An eerie green glow showed the inside of the giant frog-bin, high above his head.

That was a long drop.

Billy's sunglasses had broken in the fall, but he no longer needed them. He slipped the backpack on, then set off at a slightly downward angle to, what he hoped would be, the waste room. Despite the foul stench, the pipe was clear. He wondered what kept them so clean, then decided he didn't want to find out first hand, so he picked up the pace, holding the torch in his mouth to light the way.

Even though cats have excellent night vision, they need some light to work with. In the underground waste pipe, though, Snowy could see nothing without the orange glow from Billy's torch, which grew dimmer with each passing moment.

At first, he couldn't understand why, then he realized the batteries had started to fail. Before long, the light went out completely.

He spat the torch from his mouth, then sat down to consider his next move. *It's pitch black, but I can follow this tunnel down to the Waste Room. I'm a cat after all, my superior feline senses can guide me.* He took a dozen confident steps in the darkness, then the floor disappeared beneath him and he plunged through a gap in the pipe.

Snowy bounced off something on the way down before landing on a metal floor, ten feet below. Stunned, he lay on his side with the wind knocked out of him.

When he opened his eyes, he found he could make out his surroundings, thanks to a dim light coming from somewhere nearby. He'd landed in a large, room-sized, metal box.

Had he been able to read the blueprints Billy and Carmen studied earlier, he'd have realized he'd landed inside one of the waste compressors which crushed the park's garbage, making it easier to transport.

He looked at the thick piston which broke his fall. It ran from one end of the room to the other, then disappeared into the far wall. Light seeped in through a gap where the piston came into the compressor.

He tried to stand, but collapsed to the floor as a sharp, stabbing sensation in his right hind leg made him wince.

Not one of my better landings.

He hobbled to the hole and, with an effort, squeezed through to the other side.

The glow from the control panel in the waste room provided enough light for him to study the map Carmen had drawn.

He had less than half a mile to go. His injured leg made it hard going, but he made steady progress through the wide, well-lit passageway.

Old Tin-head will just have to give me a lift on the way back, he decided.

At last, he came to an opening. *This is it,* he

thought, I can just see the look on Razor's face when I turn up.

He limped inside to find himself in the corner of a large, dim-lit area, about sixty feet across and twenty feet deep. The floor sloped down to three display rooms, each with observation windows stretched across their width. The rooms themselves stood in complete darkness. At the far end of the viewing section, a wooden door stood slightly ajar. A bright light shone through from the other side.

The smell of disinfectant covered up any other scents, but he felt certain he'd found the unauthorized laboratory, and at least one human was nearby. As he hobbled to the nearest window, he became aware of a strange, whining noise from outside in the main corridor. It grew steadily louder, then stopped, replaced a moment later by the unmistakable echo of approaching footsteps.

Ignoring the pain, Snowy flung himself across the room, diving through the gap in the door and into the laboratory, just as someone entered the viewing area behind him.

The human followed him, pushing the door fully open with his foot.

Snowy caught a sudden whiff of coffee. He limped across the room to hide beneath the workbench against the far wall. He couldn't see much aside from the bare, concrete floor and the human's black trousers, but at least he hadn't been spotted.

Keeping to the wall, he made his way to the far corner, where he considered his next move. What was a human doing in the lab at this time of night?

A moment later, he nearly jumped out of his fur when a telephone rang on the desk above his head.

The black trousers walked toward him.

"Hello? No, this is Gladstone… You want it now? Well, okay, give me a minute to close up first."

Gladstone grabbed something from the workbench, then walked away. A few seconds later, he switched off the light and left, closing the door behind him.

Snowy's eyes dilated to make the most of the tiny light from beneath the lab door. The back of the lab now lay in total darkness.

He hobbled across the floor to squint at the small, round doorknob. *If it had a proper handle, I might have opened it.*

He remembered the animal displays above ground had a sliding panel at the bottom of their entrance doors, for putting food through. Billy had said it made the rooms look like prison cells. Dr. Euston had explained how, behind each door, a narrow access corridor led to a separate room, where the vets could examine the animals when needed.

With only his whiskers to guide him, he felt his way along the outer wall. Sure enough, he found an opening. The air felt different here. He made his way down the corridor until he came to a door.

After several seconds of ineffective struggling, he realized the food panel must have a bolt. Once he had it opened, he pushed up the metal panel, holding it above his head with both front paws. After the darkness, the glow from the viewing room shone through the cell's window like bright sunlight. He closed his eyes to avoid its glare. With his nose overloaded with chemical odors from the laboratory, he couldn't tell what, if anything, was in the room.

He stuck his head through the gap. "Pssst, Razor, you in here?"

He heard scuffling noises. The light through the window still dazzled him, but he didn't need his eyes to recognize the sound of dozens of small creatures scuttling toward him through the darkness.

Blind instinct saved him. He flung himself backward as the two nearest rats leaped at his throat. The panel slid shut with a dull thud, crushing the head of the second one. He opened his claws to slash at the only rat to make it through the gap. It was dead before it hit the floor.

The squashed rat's head kept the panel wedged open. On the other side of the door, more rats threw themselves at it, trying to force their way through. Snowy clawed at the dead body, trying to shove it back into the cell, but it wouldn't move.

He changed tactics. With a hiss of pain, he stood on his hind legs to push on the metal plate with all his might. On either side of the dead rodent's head, sharp teeth snapped at him.

He put all his weight on his injured leg and used his good hind paw to claw at their faces. His forelegs ached from the strain, but to stop pushing meant certain death.

The panel bounced upward. He let out a terrified hiss as the dead rat's head disappeared back into the room, and with a harsh clank of metal on concrete, the panel slid shut.

For once, he felt glad of the darkness. With trembling paws, he slid the bolt home, then slumped back against the door. He tried to regain his composure, but the muffled sounds of tearing flesh from the other room did nothing to help his shredded nerves.

"So," he muttered, his voice shaking, "we don't want to choose door number one then."

It took several minutes to summon the courage to try the next room, but in the end he drew back the bolt and raised the panel a fraction. When nothing attacked, he let it close again, then took off his backpack. His injured leg hurt worse than ever now.

He opened the panel again. "Anyone home?" No answer, but over the noise of the rats next door, a gentle snoring sound came from the far corner.

"Oi, Tin-head. Wake up, the cavalry's here."

Still no reply.

Maybe they drugged him.

He shoved his backpack in ahead of him, then slid through the gap. As he dragged himself through, the metal panel raked across his injured leg. With a squeal of pain, he jerked it out of harm's way. The panel slid shut with an ominous clang.

He licked at the wound for a while, then a feeling of dread came over him. He looked up. Something had changed, but what?

He'd been facing the door. A voice in his head told him to turn around, but he didn't dare. A chilled knot twisted around inside his stomach.

The snoring had stopped.

He forced himself to look.

In the far corner, he saw the outline of an enormous animal against the window.

That's a darn sight bigger than a fox.

He scrabbled at the door panel, but it wouldn't open. At the sound of the creature shuffling across the floor toward him, he redoubled his efforts. It slid open half-an-inch, then stuck fast.

The beast was right behind him now. He could hear its ragged breath. He gave up on the panel and turned back to face his adversary. "Stay away from me. I mean it. I may look small, but I fight like a demon."

It peered at him through the gloom.

Snowy's whiskers bent back beneath the creature's musky, banana breath. It loomed over him, mouth open.

Snowy became acutely aware of some very large, white teeth. Fear turned to anger. He let out a sharp hiss. If he had to die, at least he'd go down fighting. "Back off, pal. I'm warning you, back home they call me The Little Tiger."

The monster seemed to consider this for a moment. "Oh really," it said. "They call *me* Mr. Tinkles."

Chapter Thirteen
From Bad to Worse

Billy woke to the sound of his mother, drawing open his bedroom curtains. "Up you get, sleepyhead. We've a busy day ahead. Church first, then Aggie invited us to the opening of the new Sea View area at *Adventure Safari*." She glanced around his room. "Strange, I haven't seen Snowy all morning. It's not like that cat of yours to miss breakfast."

When his mother left, Billy got ready. He wasn't too worried about Snowy, the only escape route from the tunnels went through the staff car park, which he couldn't use until the security people opened the doors for the morning shift.

At breakfast, Emma managed to get cereal in her hair. The resulting bath put them behind schedule and almost made them late for church again.

Helen Roberts overtook them at the church doors. "Just in time," she grinned. "I should have played the opening bars of *All Things Bright and Beautiful* about twenty seconds ago." She practically galloped up the aisle, reaching the organ just as Reverend Loampit announced the opening hymn.

Billy couldn't help noticing the giant of a man next to Carmen and Aggie in the front row. "I bet that's Benedict Barnum. Carmen says he funded the park."

His father stopped singing to answer. "He's a generous bloke. Aggie says he just paid to have the church roof repaired."

"What a kind man." Mrs. Euston kept a wary eye on little Emma, who insisted on standing by herself, with her own hymn book, though she still held it upside-down.

During the second hymn, Carmen turned to look at Billy and mouthed "Any news?"

He shook his head.

After the service, Aggie and Carmen went straight to the front gate with Mr. Barnum and drove off in an enormous, gold-colored limo. Billy wandered over to talk to Marcus, but Reverend Loampit intercepted him.

"William, my boy. How are you? And how's my old friend Snowy this morning?"

"Fine thanks, Reverend Lump– I mean, Loampit. How do you know Snowy?"

The vicar grinned. "Oh, he comes over to my house most Saturdays. I usually have roast chicken for lunch. He eats the leftovers while I practice my sermon on him. I can always tell how much re-writing I need to do, by the amount of food he leaves on the plate when he makes a run for it."

Billy's nose felt itchy, he stuck his hands in his pockets, looking for a tissue. "I shouldn't think it would help. Snowy wouldn't let twenty minutes of boredom put him off his dinner. Not that your sermons are boring," he added. "I mean, I enjoyed your talk about, er…" He felt his cheeks flame as he struggled to recall the subject of the morning's lesson.

Loampit gave him a friendly slap on the back.

"You're a rotten liar, lad, but I appreciate the thought. Cast your eyes about you for a moment."

Billy looked around. The villagers had spread out around the church grounds in small groups, chatting to each other.

Loampit put an arm around his shoulder. "When I first came here from Ireland, I couldn't believe my luck to find the church so full every week. Then it dawned on me. In a small village like this, there's no better place than the Sunday church service to catch up on all the local gossip. I'll bet you a pound to a penny, not one in ten of these good people could tell you the subject of today's sermon. Still, the way I see it, as long as they keep coming through those doors, I get a shot at their ears, and every now and then, I can make a little difference." He handed Billy a carrier bag. "Speaking of which, these are for you."

The bag felt heavy. Inside he found a thick wad of comic books, each wrapped in a clear plastic envelope. He pulled one out. "Spiderman. Wow, this looks really old."

Loampit beamed. "A first edition. I've had these since I was your age. They'd fetch a pretty penny, if I ever sold them, so I'd rather you didn't let young Emma get at them."

"I won't," Billy said, grinning from ear to ear. "And thanks."

Mr. Tinkles sat in his cell, licking his lips. He'd never tasted anything quite like this before. He wondered how something so small could be so crunchy. A tiny part of it had wedged in his front teeth. It took several minutes of patient work before he finally managed to dislodge it with his tongue. "A very unusual flavor, but quite delicious."

His guest grinned. "Cheese-and-Onion, my personal favorite. I said you'd like 'em. Here you go, mate, have another."

Snowy sat beside Mr. Tinkles with his back to the cell door. After the initial confusion, the gorilla had apologized profusely for any misunderstanding. He'd assured Snowy he wasn't about to be eaten or even dismembered. Even so it took quite a while for Snowy's heart rate to settle down to a reasonable level, and even longer to get Mr. Tinkles to understand his name wasn't really 'The Little Tiger'.

Mr. Tinkles listened in silence while Snowy explained how he'd woken up after a lifesaving operation with the ability to understand human speak and how, apart from Billy, no other humans could understand what *he* said. Snowy told him all about Fur-Face, and why it was very important he found Razor, then report back, so the evil man could be stopped.

"That's pretty much it really." Snowy squinted into the gloom, trying to see his new friend's face. "So, what do you think? Can you help?"

The gorilla scratched his armpits before answering. "So, you're really called Snowy then?"

"Yes." Snowy let out a deep sigh. He had a feeling this was going to be a long night.

"But you're a black cat, right?"

"Yes."

During another long pause. Snowy imagined he

could hear the gorilla's lips moving as he tried to process the information. After a while, he took pity on the gentle giant.

"Don't worry, Mr. T. It's ironic."

"What is?"

"My name."

"But you said it was Snowy."

Snowy's head slumped back against the metal panel. "Tell you what. Why don't I get us some more grub?" He fumbled in his backpack for the last packet of crispy snacks. "Mr. Tinkles, do you think you could open the panel on this door?"

"It wouldn't do any good, Ironic, er…Snowy. I'd never fit through."

"Yeah…right, but I can. I want to check the cell next door."

Mr. Tinkles lifted the panel with ease.

Snowy limped through the opening. He found the next door easily enough, but the bolt holding the panel in place proved too stiff for him to move. He scratched at the metal with his claws.

"You in there, Tin-head?"

From the other side of the door, a muffled voice answered. "Snowy? How did you get here?"

"I came to find you. I can't open this panel, the bolt's stuck." He explained Billy's plan. "Only, now I can't get out."

"You have to," Razor said. "I heard them talking. They're putting on a display tomorrow. Something about 'David and Goliath'. I don't what it means, but I doubt it's good."

"I've heard of them," Snowy said. "From the old

vicar up at the village church, the one who keeps trying to get me to join the priesthood. This bully called Goliath kept picking on this short kid, named David." Snowy scrabbled at the back of his memory for more information. "David got fed up with it and challenged him to a fight after school. Everybody turned up to watch. I can't remember any more, except the winner got promoted to Chief Shepherd. Does that help at all?"

After a short pause, Razor's muffled voice answered. "They want me to fight. Fur-Face's rats are a lot smaller than me. The humans have never actually seen me kill one. They must want a display."

Snowy thought about the five-hundred-pound giant, currently eating crispy snacks in the next room and reached his own conclusion, but kept it to himself. "Listen, I can't stay out here. I'm going to hide in the lab. I'll make a break for it when they open the door tomorrow." He didn't add how much his wounded leg would make this difficult.

As he started back along the corridor, Razor called out again. "Snowy?"

"Yeah, I'm still here."

"You found my family. Thank you."

I never imagined I'd live to hear him say those words, Snowy thought. Too bad *he* won't live to see them again. He tapped on the metal panel. "Anytime, mate, anytime."

"Did you find your friend?" Mr. Tinkles asked, after he let Snowy back in. "Didn't he want to come and visit?"

Snowy helped himself to the last crispy snack. "I couldn't unbolt his door." He squinted through the gloom at the giant ape. This doesn't make sense. He tried to imagine an angry Mr. Tinkles, but it seemed about as believable as a homicidal butterfly.

"Mr. T, do gorillas fight at all?"

"Oh my goodness no. We hardly ever indulge in that kind of thing, except to challenge for leadership, or protect the group. Even then, we usually just stand up tall and make unkind comments about the shape of our opponent's nose. If those don't work, we thump our chests a lot. That usually does the trick."

"It would certainly work on me," Snowy relaxed a little. The humans must know about gorillas. Perhaps they meant for Razor to fight rats after all.

"Except if something *really* upsets us," Mr. Tinkles added, "then we break its back and pull off its arms and legs."

Snowy's heart sank. "Oh. Tell me something. How do you feel about foxes?"

"Can't say I've ever met one."

"Well, my friend next door is a fox, and I've a nasty feeling the humans want you to fight him tomorrow."

"Oh dear, I don't think I'd like that."

"Good, 'cause the way I see it, when I tell Razor about you, he won't want to fight either. So, long as you both agree to just sit there and do nothing, we shouldn't have a problem."

"Best tell him not to look me in the eye," Mr. Tinkles said. "We gorillas consider it extremely bad form. I've been known to get pretty sarcastic about it in the past."

"No problem. Could you open this panel again, I want to explain things to my friend, then I'm going back

170

to hide in the lab. I'll make a break for it first thing tomorrow. With any luck, I should be back with the cavalry before things get nasty."

"Cavalry?"

When Snowy explained, Mr. Tinkles clapped his hands together. "Oh won't that be nice. I've always loved horses."

Snowy went to tell Razor the plan, taking special care to emphasize the part about not looking Mr. Tinkles in the eye, then made his way back to the lab.

He curled up on the cold floor beneath the desk. The laboratory smells and his aching leg made it difficult to relax, but he eventually drifted off. He dreamed of sheep, looked after by a gorilla shepherd, with the help of a trusty sheep-fox.

Several hours later, Snowy was quite literally jerked out of his sleep as something pulled him out from beneath the table by the scruff of his neck.

"Gladstone! How dare you bring a pet into my laboratory?"

Startled, Snowy struggled to get free, but could only dangle, helpless in the human's grip. He found himself hoisted in the air, facing Gladstone, who hurried through from the next room.

"I don't understand, Farofas. I don't have a pet."

Now I'm in for it, Snowy thought. I'll be sitting in a cell, wearing me own private satellite dish before you can say 'pass the catnip'. He let his body go limp.

Farofas examined him with disgust. "Get the door."

Gladstone held open the lab door as Farofas, still holding the cat out in front of him, strode across the floor. Snowy couldn't believe his luck. *The landing's going to hurt like hell, but at least I'll be outside.*

In the doorway, Farofas swung his arm in a wide arc. Snowy allowed his body to go limp, in preparation for a painful landing, but at the last moment Farofas stopped his swing and held him up for re-examination.

"You know, this animal looks familiar."

The assistant peered at Snowy. "I don't think so. Wait, yes, this is the animal Mrs. Cranbrook forced you to operate on back in-aaargh!"

Snowy decided attack was the best form of defense. He swiped his claw across Gladstone's nose.

The injured man let out a high-pitched squeal and leaped backward, clutching at his face. Snowy wriggled around, clawing at the hand holding him, but couldn't quite reach it.

"Stop fussing, man. Fetch me a container."

With one hand over his nose, Gladstone ran to the corner of the lab and pulled a large cat box from the shelf.

At the sight of it, ice-cold terror welled up inside Snowy. "You're not getting me in there!" He couldn't break free as Farofas carried him across the room toward his worst nightmare.

Gladstone set the box on the table.

Snowy screeched with the pain from his injured leg as he stretched out all four paws to grip the edges of the box, making himself too wide to fit in. Terror gave him unnatural strength and after a few seconds of scrabbling, he even managed to knock the container to the floor.

"We'll have to sedate him," Farofas said. "Bring me the MASC." He shook Snowy like a rag doll, then held him out toward his assistant, who picked up a spray can.

Gladstone pointed the canister at the cat's face, but just as he pressed the nozzle, Snowy lashed out with his good hind leg to kick the MASC out of the human's hand. Instead of coming straight at him, the spray went up in the air. Gladstone rolled his eyes and slumped to the floor.

Snowy redoubled his efforts to escape, but the room was spinning now. He no longer had control over his body. Within seconds, he could barely twitch. A hand stretched out in front of him to pick the cat box from the floor. Terrified now, he tried to scream for Billy, Razor, anyone, but the MASC spray had numbed his throat. He could only watch in mute horror, as Farofas lowered him into the mouth of container.

Once inside, he tried to curl himself up into a ball, but his numb limbs wouldn't obey. He stared up from the base of the cat box as Farofas closed the lid. He wanted it to be over. He wanted to die. Then finally, thankfully, he passed out.

Chapter Fourteen
Rats

Colored flags on silver poles fluttered in the summer breeze above *Adventure Safari*, as the Euston family enjoyed their lunch with Aggie and Carmen at the newly-opened Dolphin Diner.

"I invited an old friend of mine, Benedict Barnum, to join us," Aggie said. "You probably saw him at church earlier. Benny's the main financial backer for both the park and the research center. I've asked him to open the Sea View area for us. I wonder where he's got to."

After the meal, a waiter hurried over with a whispered message for Aggie. She listened closely, then smiled across the table at Billy and Carmen.

"It seems a couple of youngsters called in sick and can't be here for the show. We need two people to take their places in the parade. Any volunteers?"

Carmen jumped out of her chair. "Come on, Bill, it's loads of fun. I took part in it last year, when they opened the Jungle Trek log ride. I got to be a baby tiger."

Billy didn't really want to go, but thought it would seem rude to refuse. He followed Carmen to the underground tunnels, to collect their costumes.

"I would have liked something a little more exciting

than this," Carmen said, looking at the tortoise outfit she wore. She burst out laughing when she saw Billy. "You look like Toad of Toad Hall."

"I feel like a twit," Billy said. He tried to look at his feet, but thick layers of green foam around his waist prevented him. "Why do I have to be the frog?"

"The flippers were too big for me. Come on, that whistle is the two-minute warning before the parade."

They took their places beside a giant alligator float. Rock music hammered out over the P.A. system as the parade came out of the tunnel on the western perimeter. It proceeded down the park's central lane, toward the new Sea View buildings, more than a mile away.

Each section of *Adventure Safari* had its own float. Juggling stilt-walkers, wearing bright-colored outfits, weaved in and out of the procession. Painted clowns threw foam pies at each other, cheered on by the delighted crowds lining the route. Alongside each float, people dressed in animal costumes handed out small toys and candy to excited children.

The sun blazed down on them. Inside his frog-suit, Billy began to sweat.

"Amazing isn't it?" Carmen shouted to make herself heard above the din. When Billy didn't answer, she waved her hand in front of his face. "Earth to Frog-boy, anyone home?"

"Sorry, I can't stop thinking about Snowy. I expected him back by the time I got home from church, but he didn't show up. To tell you the truth, I'm a little worried."

"He'll be fine," Carmen yelled. "The lab would have been empty at that time of night."

"I suppose so." Billy paused to press a bag of Crocodile Snappy Snacks into the outstretched hand of a cheering toddler. "I've a horrible feeling he's in trouble." A trickle of sweat ran down his spine. "I need a soda."

They walked to the side of the alligator float, where Billy gratefully accepted the two bottles someone handed him from inside the reptile's canvas belly.

"Tell you what," Carmen shouted. "We'll look for him after the parade? We can slip away from the others on the way back and borrow one of those electric people carriers."

Billy drained his half-pint bottle in one go. "What if someone sees us?"

"Just act confident. On a busy day like this, nobody will give us a second glance."

Billy wasn't entirely certain a toad and a tortoise, driving an electric car down an underground tunnel, would pass without comment or suspicion, but he couldn't shake off the nagging feeling that Snowy needed him. "Okay."

"I bet we don't find him," Carmen added, as she grabbed a fresh bucket of giveaway goodies from the helper inside the float, "He's probably back at your house right now, relaxing in front of the TV."

When Snowy came to, he found himself still in the cat box, which had been turned the right way up and set on a table. The stench of antiseptic made his eyes water. The plastic walls closed in around him. He curled into a ball and lay there, trembling.

From somewhere out of sight, he heard a deep, powerful voice. He couldn't see the newcomer, but he could tell how nervous it made his captors.

"What's going on here?"

Despite his fear, Snowy allowed himself an inner smile at the sight of the huge, white plaster on Gladstone's nose.

Farofas pointed at him. "We discovered an intruder, Mr. Barnum. This vicious animal attacked my assistant."

Barnum's face appeared at the cat box door. He looked surprised to see Snowy.

"I expected an escaped leopard, or perhaps a baby crocodile, but not a cat."

"This is not just any cat," Farofas said. "This is the animal Mrs. Cranbrook forced me to operate on. I wasted an entire batch of enhanced Propofol, just to save its worthless life."

"Oh yes, I remember her e-mails on the subject." Barnum frowned at Snowy. "You caused me a lot of trouble, little fellow. Once Aggie decided she didn't want my pet scientist around, we had to move our operation here."

Snowy tried to hiss at the big man, but it came out as a gasp.

Barnum straightened up. "I left the Russian delegation in the viewing room. I trust everything is prepared."

Farofas practically bowed. "Yes, sir. The fox has been well looked after and the gorilla placed in the adjoining cell, as you instructed."

"Excellent. Vladimir's people took care of General Gomez for me. He seemed most upset when I told him about your little side venture. For your sake, I hope he's impressed with the demonstration."

Snowy heard a scratchy, rasping noise, then gagged at the stench of cigar smoke which suddenly filled the air.

"Put our little friend here in with the overgrown chimpanzee. He can give your trained fox a warm-up before the big match."

Gladstone carried Snowy's box around to the back of the cells. He opened the top half of Mr. Tinkles's door, then tipped Snowy out onto the concrete floor. "Die slowly, cat."

The top of the cell door slammed shut behind him. With an effort he pulled himself into a sitting position. His hind leg felt numb.

The room seemed brighter than it had the night before. For the first time, he got a clear look at Mr. Tinkles, who sat slouched in the corner, with his back to the door. "Hello again, Mr. T."

Mr. Tinkles clapped his massive hands in delight. "Snowy!" His face fell. "No horses?"

Wary of eye contact, Snowy focused on the gorilla's huge chest. "Sorry, they couldn't make it."

In the viewing room, the Russian businessmen watched through the window of the adjoining cell as Farofas put Razor through his paces.

When the demonstration finished, Barnum addressed the delegation. "Gentlemen, what you have just seen will revolutionize the entertainment industry in your country. For some time now, I've been lobbying the Russian government for permission to build a string of sports arenas throughout your country."

The leader of the Russians spoke. "We know this,

Mr. Barnum. If you Americans had your way, our country would be littered with baseball parks and fast food restaurants."

Barnum laughed. "My dear Vladimir, who said anything about 'human' sport." He spread out his huge arms. "No, sir. I propose to build dozens of small stadia, each holding no more than ten thousand spectators, who will enjoy the most incredible animal entertainment in the history of the world."

He leaned back against the window. "Dog fighting is immensely popular in your country. Imagine the financial benefits for someone who could stage these fights in the proper surroundings. Picture it, gentlemen. Giant screens showing close-ups and slow-motion replays of the action."

He gestured at Farofas. "With the device you've just seen, we could stage fights between all manner of God's creatures." Barnum stopped in front of Vladimir and lowered his voice. "Can't you just see it? Tigers facing off against alligators, elephants against bears, all for the enjoyment of ten thousand excited onlookers, each one gambling their hard-earned rubles on the winner. Why, there hasn't been a spectacle like it since the days of the Roman Empire."

Farofas held out a tray. Barnum picked up a small microchip from it. "With these tiny implants, we can make an animal attack whatever we choose. Hell, you could even set up a little black market entertainment, using human contestants, if you wanted."

Vladimir's lips pulled back in a cruel smile. "What you suggest has a certain appeal, but even dog fighting is illegal in Russia."

"At the moment, yes," Barnum said, "but it still goes on. The police on the scene take their bribes and enjoy the show."

One of the other Russians spoke. "They could not turn a blind eye to an entire stadium. Our government would be hounded into action by the western liberal press."

Barnum grinned. "'Hounded', very witty. But what if it became legal? After all, the Spanish have their bullrings, the British their fox hunting. Why shouldn't Mother Russia enjoy its dog fights?"

"I do not believe our government would lift the restrictions," Vladimir said.

Barnum threw back his head and laughed. "Do you really think I'd go to all this trouble without first making sure I had the proper connections. My friends in the Russian Federal Assembly have already drafted the necessary bill. Your Government will vote it through by the end of the year."

"You seem to have thought of everything, Mr. Barnum." Vladimir stared through the window at Razor. "But we have yet to see a demonstration of your animal in combat."

"Of course," Barnum took a long puff at his cigar, then gestured to Gladstone. "Turn up the light in the gorilla's cell."

Barnum stepped to the window and rapped on the glass. Mr. Tinkles looked at him. Barnum chuckled to himself, as if at some private joke. "So long, big guy. Enjoy your retirement." He held the gorilla's gaze for several seconds, then blew a mouthful of cigar smoke at the window.

Mr. Tinkles let out a deep growl. "What a rude man. We haven't even been introduced and he's looking me straight in the eye as if we'd known each other for years." Without warning, he leaped to the window and pounded his fists against the glass, which rattled like a thunderclap, but did not break.

In the viewing room, everyone jumped back, except for Barnum, who just stood there, smiling. He took a last puff at his cigar, then dropped the butt on the floor, symbolically crushing it beneath his foot. He turned back to the Russians with a smile. "Now, I'm afraid I must go. I have to officially open the newest section of this park so I'll leave you in the capable hands of Doctor Farofas. We've arranged a demonstration which should leave you in no doubt as to the potential of our new technology." He looked at Gladstone. "Make sure you record this. Have the video transmitted directly to my private laptop."

As Barnum left the viewing room, Mr. Tinkles yelled at his retreating back. "Your hair needs a trim, human, and I certainly wouldn't wear those shoes with that color tie if I were you!"

He shuffled back to join Snowy, who stared, open-mouthed, at the window, where the mist from the gorilla's breath had begun to evaporate. "Wow."

"I'm so sorry you had to hear that kind of talk, Snowy, but I needed to put the vulgar fellow in his place."

A strange whirring noise made them both jump. On the side wall of the cell, a small panel slid open. A moment later, the aerial on Razor's helmet appeared, closely followed by Razor himself. As soon as he'd squeezed through the gap, the panel closed behind him.

He looked at Snowy in surprise. "I thought you'd be long gone."

"They made me an offer I couldn't refuse."

Mr. Tinkles clapped his hands in delight. "A unicorn, how delightful."

"What? No, I'm a fox." Razor turned to face Mr. Tinkles. "Bloody hell, you must be Goliath." Just in time, he remembered to avoid eye contact. He trotted over to Snowy. "Why does he think I'm a unicorn?"

"It must be your antennae. I didn't know Fur-Face had given you a new helmet."

"I wish he hadn't. He can use it to send pain signals into my head."

Snowy looked into the viewing room. "I guess they'll want to start their little show soon, but if we all stay calm and nobody looks Mr. T. in the eye, we should be fine."

Razor looked uncomfortable. "I'm not so sure. Fur-Face wants me to kill you first, then go for the gorilla's throat."

Mr. Tinkles covered his mouth with giant hands. "What an absolute rotter."

"Fight the urge." Snowy limped to Mr. Tinkles, making sure the gorilla stood between himself and the fox. "Remember, I have total faith in you."

"He's getting angry," Razor said. "When he hits the pain switch, I'll either have to kill you, or get my brains fried."

As Snowy and Mr. Tinkles looked on, Razor's eyes rolled into the back of his head. He collapsed to the floor, his body twitching back and forth in violent spasms, then went limp.

The fox lay still, panting, then glowered at Snowy. "If I don't kill you, he'll hit the pain switch again." He let out a sharp yelp as another spasm took hold. This one lasted longer than the first.

Mr. Tinkles leaned down to whisper in Snowy's ear. "Tell him to attack. I'll catch him before he gets to you."

"Yeah, right. Let's do that…not."

"Trust me," Mr. Tinkles said. "I can do this."

A few feet away, Razor lay sprawled out on the concrete floor, gasping.

"Bloody hell," Snowy groaned. "Why didn't I leave town when I had the chance? Oi, Tin-head, make your move. Mr. T. says he'll catch you before you get to me." Their eyes met, but Razor seemed not to understand. Snowy shook his head. "He can't hear me. He's in too much pain."

"You'll have to provoke him."

"I don't know how. I could try singing. He hates that. No, we don't want to make him too angry. Hang on, I've got it." He leaned across the gorilla's giant leg to yell at Razor. "I suppose this would be a bad time to tell you Scala had company when I saw her the other day. And I don't mean your cubs."

"Be quiet," Razor hissed.

"I must say, we had a bit of an awkward moment when I peeped through the fence."

"Shut up!"

"But then, how was I to know I'd catch them '*Asti Spumanti*' so to speak."

"Liar!" With a snarl, Razor dived across the room.

"Mr. Teeeeee!"

Snowy felt Razor's hot breath on his neck as a mouthful of sharp teeth snapped together a claw's width from his throat. When he dared open his eyes he saw Mr. Tinkles holding the enraged animal above his head. " Nice one, Mr. T. I never doubted you for a moment. Now what?"

The electric whining sound started again. This time it came from the opposite wall. Frantic scrabbling sounds from behind the panel drowned out the hum of the motor.

"Rats," Snowy yelled. "Get me over there, quick."

Still holding the struggling fox above his head, Mr. Tinkles scooped up Snowy with his foot and sent him sliding across the floor.

The panel had already begun to open as Snowy reached it. The first rats charged into the room. His sharp claws easily took care of them, but dozens more poured through the opening, scrambling over each other in their haste to get at him.

He fell backward beneath three large rats. Just then, a huge black foot crashed down beside his head. Still holding Razor above his head, Mr. Tinkles stamped on the other rodents, crushing them with ease.

"Put me down. I'm okay, he's using the pain on the rats now."

Mr. Tinkles dropped Razor to the floor, and together they fought their attackers back.

"Stuff the bodies into the gap," Snowy shouted. "Squeeze them in as tight as you can. It'll buy us some time."

Mr. Tinkles scooped up a handful of dead and dying rodents, then mashed them into the opening. A few seconds later, Razor snapped the neck of the last rat in their cell. They all flopped to the ground, exhausted.

Snowy's injured leg felt like it was on fire. Blood oozed from dozens of small bites all over his body. Razor hadn't fared much better. Mr. Tinkles sat in the middle of the room to examine a few cuts on his feet, but otherwise looked unhurt.

"Now what?" Razor panted. They could hear unpleasant crunching sounds from the next room. "It won't take them long to gnaw through the bodies. How many are in there?"

Snowy lay on his side, sucking in air. The stench of blood and death filled his nostrils. He felt exhausted, but strangely exhilarated. "I reckon we killed about twenty, but judging from the noise in there, I'd say there's plenty more."

"Do you think the cavalry will come soon?" Mr. Tinkles asked.

Snowy let out a hollow laugh. "They never got their invitation. We've about two minutes before those rats clear the hole. We just about stopped them last time. I don't know if we can do it again."

Mr. Tinkles stared at the floor. "I don't think I like the sound of that."

Outside in the viewing room, Farofas removed his metal helmet. He stood with Gladstone, a little way along the window, pressing buttons on the remote control device in his hand.

The dead bodies wedged into the opening began to move.

"It won't be long now," Razor said. He looked at Snowy. "For what it's worth, I'm sorry I dragged you into this."

Snowy didn't answer right away. He stared at Razor's helmet with a peculiar smile on his face. "Hang on a minute, lads. I've got a great idea."

Chapter Fifteen
Glass, Bullets and Giant Frogs

Fur-Face watched the frenzied efforts of his rats with a satisfied smile. "Now the bloodlust is upon them, my rodent army will soon tear their way through to the other cell. Even the gorilla will be ripped to pieces."

"Doctor Farofas," Vladimir said. "How much control do you have over these rats?"

"They don't have microchips in their heads, although I've had some success in that area. We've chemically suppressed the serotonin nerve cells in their brains. This makes them extremely aggressive. They will attack any other creature without warning."

Vladimir looked puzzled. "Then why do you need your remote control?"

"To adjust a high-pitched frequency in the rodents' cell. The sound causes acute distress and provides them with the proper motivation to escape into the other room. But I must take care. Too much stimulation will drive them insane. They would simply turn on each other."

One of the other Russians grinned. "It seems to effect the monkey and his friends too."

Farofas stepped back to look through the window at the three animals huddled together in the middle of the gorilla's cell. "Perhaps they're discussing a survival strategy."

The Russians laughed.

Mr. Tinkles had his back to the window. They watched him pick up Razor and hold him in his lap. His broad back blocked their view, but they all heard the crack as something snapped in his hands.

Vladimir chuckled. "The gorilla thinks the fox will make a better plug than dead rats."

Razor's broken antennae clattered to the floor as Mr. Tinkles came to the window. Blood dripped from a cut in his hand when he reached up to hold the top of Razor's head against the toughened glass.

Snowy had to shout to make himself heard above the din from the next cell. "Be careful with my friend there."

Mr. Tinkles grunted in acknowledgement, then pushed the sharp stump of Razor's broken antennae into the window.

"Good," Snowy yelled. "Now, make a big moon shape, and try to remember he's not an owl. Razor won't thank you if you twist his neck all the way around."

Razor kept very quiet, focusing all his efforts on keeping his neck and spine rigid. Holding the fox in his paws like an oversized, furry crayon, Mr. Tinkles cut a wide circle in the window.

In the observation room, the humans clapped their hands over their ears to shut out the awful screeching sound of metal on glass. The teeth-jarring noise provoked the rats into an even greater frenzy.

"Hurry," Snowy yelled. "They'll be through at any moment."

Mr. Tinkles finished the circle, then scraped a large

'X' through it. He lumbered back to the rear wall, scooping up Snowy on the way.

The dead bodies blocking the entrance seemed to come to life as rats flooded into the cell. In the viewing room, the Russians' smug grins vanished. They drew guns from inside their jackets.

"Here we go," Mr. Tinkles shouted. He tucked Snowy and Razor under each arm, then bounded across the floor, squashing some of the approaching rats beneath his feet. A moment later he shoulder-charged the X in the circle.

Accompanied by the deafening roar of gunfire and shattered glass, Mr. Tinkles went through the window like a fur-covered wrecking ball. Clutching Snowy and Razor to him, he rolled over on his shoulder ending up standing in front of Farofas, who fell to his knees in abject terror.

Alarm bells sounded.

Vladimir shoved Gladstone against the wall. "Get us out of here now, or you die."

Gladstone looked past the Russian at Farofas, now groveling at the feet of the gorilla. "Follow me, gentlemen."

Mr. Tinkles placed Snowy and Razor on the floor, then drew himself up to his full height, pounding his chest with anvil-like fists. "You naughty man," he roared. "How dare you try to hurt my friends?" He dragged Farofas to his feet.

"Don't kill me. Please don't kill me."

Mr. Tinkles shouted over the noise of the alarm bell. "Join your friends." He grabbed the back of the scientist's trousers with his free hand and tossed him

189

across the room.

Farofas threw up his arms to protect his face as he sailed over the low brick wall into the gorilla's cell, where he skidded across the concrete floor to hit the door with a loud crash.

He scrambled to his feet and tried to open the door, but it was locked from the outside. Out in the viewing room, Snowy couldn't see the rats, but he heard their frenzied squealing as they attacked. With a terrified shriek, Farofas dashed back toward the broken window, but halfway there, he fell to the floor, out of Snowy's line of sight.

His blood-chilling scream continued for several seconds, then suddenly stopped. Moments later, a hand appeared at the base of the window. Bloodied fingers clawed at the jagged stumps of broken glass along the low wall. After a few seconds they went limp, then slipped back out of sight.

The alarm bell stopped ringing.

Snowy found himself wishing for some other noise to drown out the sound coming from the other room.

Mr. Tinkles stomped on Fur-Face's remote control. He tossed the remains through the shattered window. "I bet he wishes rats were more like gorillas." He slumped back against the wall and slid to a sitting position. "All in all, I'd say everything went pretty much according to the plan. Wouldn't you agree?"

"I guess so," Snowy panted. He tried to stand, but his legs gave way beneath him. "But I still like my idea better."

Mr. Tinkles gestured to where Razor lay, motionless, on the floor. "Is your friend all right?"

"I dunno," Snowy felt woozy. His vision went blurred. "You all right, Razor?"

"He's still breathing," Mr. Tinkles said. "I'm sure he's okay. What's the matter?"

Snowy stared at the dark stain, spreading out across the viewing room carpet from beneath Mr. Tinkles. "Well, someone isn't. Where's all that coming from?"

"Ah. I'm afraid that would be me."

Snowy laughed with relief. "Now I know how you got your name."

Mr. Tinkles gave a weak smile. "I'm afraid you're mistaken."

For the first time, Snowy noticed the three large holes in the gorilla's chest. "You never said you were hurt."

"I don't like to make a fuss." The gorilla's head fell back against the wall with a thud.

"Wait right there." Snowy dragged himself through the open laboratory door. A short while later he returned, pushing the lab's first aid kit in front of him. When he reached Mr. Tinkles, he pried open the lid and fished around inside.

"There you go." He dropped a wad of gauze into the gorilla's lap. "Push this against one of the holes to slow the bleeding. That's what the humans do. I'll find some more."

He dug out a second roll, but when he turned back, the gorilla hadn't moved. His eyes had closed. A gnawing sense of dread crept over him. "Oh no. Come on, Mr. T. Stay with me. You'll miss the cavalry if you die now."

Snowy climbed onto his friend's chest to listen for a

heartbeat. It was there, but faint.

"Snowy?" The gorilla's voice was barely more than a whisper.

"Right here, Mr. T."

"Can I ask you something."

"Sure, what?"

"Is it too late to change my mind and vote for your idea?"

"That's the spirit, mate. You hang in there."

A distant humming noise came from out in the tunnels. As it grew louder, Snowy crawled out from under the gorilla's limp arm. "This could be the cavalry right now. Don't you go anywhere."

His paws squelched on the blood-soaked carpet as he staggered to the entrance, only to recoil in horror as a huge frog ran round the corner. "Bloody hell!"

The frog let out a muffled yell and pulled at its head.

Snowy collapsed to the floor. "I'm already dead." He let the blackness envelop him.

Billy threw the frog's head aside and ran to the motionless cat.

Carmen waddled into the room a few moments later. "You might have given me a hand. It's hard to stand up in this thing once you land on your back. Oh my God! What happened here?"

Billy didn't reply. He knelt on the wet carpet, cradling Snowy's blood-soaked body in his arms. "Don't just stand there, get help."

She ran toward the tunnel, but before she reached the doorway, an armed security team charged into the room.

The leader glanced at the viewing room, then signaled to one of his men. "Get the girl out of here. Now. If she hasn't already seen that, she's lucky."

Someone bundled Carmen outside. Two others went into the laboratory, while the last to arrive checked on Razor. "The fox is still breathing, Sarge."

The team leader crouched beside Billy. "Hey, son. Sorry you got here before us. A boy your age shouldn't have to see this kind of thing." He looked up. "What about the gorilla?"

The man kneeling beside Mr. Tinkles shook his head.

Billy looked at the team leader. His voice croaked. "I want my dad."

"Of course, son, I understand." The team leader spoke into his headset. "Security team Alpha-one to Base. We have a situation in the North Sector tunnel system. Location, disused presentation area. I need an ambulance and animal emergency medical team down here, ASAP."

He looked at the broken window. "I'm afraid so, sir. One fatality and two dead animals, a gorilla and a cat."

"Snowy's not dead." Billy yelled. "Tell them to get my dad. Tell them Doctor Euston is with Aggie Cranbrook at the opening ceremony. He'll know what to do."

"All right, take it easy." The Sergeant looked at Snowy's limp body. "Take him out to the mobile. We'll get him and the fox to the med-center." He helped Billy to his feet. "Jackson, go with him, and for Christ's sake, don't let him see the other room."

Jackson looked glad to have an excuse to leave. He put his arm around Billy's shoulder. "Come on, but keep your eyes on the cat, all right?"

For Billy, the next few minutes passed by in a daze. The world around him had faded into the background. He was vaguely aware of Carmen sitting next to him on the people carrier, trying to reassure him everything would be all right.

They sped through the underground tunnels, with Billy cradling Snowy in his arms until they reached the central dome.

The last few floats had just returned from the parade. Some of the cast members had already gone back to the changing areas, while others set to work dismantling the exhibits for storage.

People stopped and stared as the carrier came to a halt beside one of the topside access points, where Doctor Morton and an assistant from the animal infirmary waited for them. The assistant picked up Razor from the back of the electric car.

Dr. Morton took Snowy. "It's okay, Bill. We'll take good care of him. Your dad's getting things prepared in the park surgery. If anyone can help Snowy, he can." He turned to Carmen. "You'd best get changed. Mister Barnum had to leave, so Aggie's handling the opening ceremony by herself. She wants you to meet her there. You should get yourself cleaned up too, Bill."

"No. I'm staying with Snowy," Billy said. "He'll be scared if he wakes up on his own."

Dr. Morton looked over Billy's shoulder. "I think you're wanted here."

Billy turned to see his mother, fighting her way

through the crowd. A look of horror flashed across her face when she saw the fresh blood, splattered across the front of his outfit.

"It's all right, Mom." He fought back tears. "Not my blood...Snowy's." He choked back the boulder in his throat. "Oh, Mom. I think he's going to die."

She wrapped her arms around him, scolding him through her tears. "What were you thinking? Why would you run off like that? The parade manager said you and Carmen took one of the underground cars." She pulled back to study her son's face, then hugged him again, even tighter. "Never mind. You're safe, that's the important thing."

"I'm okay. I sent Snowy down here to check something out for us. When he didn't come back, we went to look for him, but Carmen and I were never in any danger, honest."

Mrs. Euston brushed his hair with her fingers. "Well," she sniffed, "let's get you cleaned up. You look like you've been dissected."

Twenty minutes later, Billy sat next to his mother in the reception area of the park surgery, Aggie and Carmen sat across from them.

The minutes dragged by.

Aggie broke the silence. "Louise, dear, where's little Emma?"

Mrs. Euston allowed herself a little smile. "Back at the Dolphin Diner. Helen volunteered to look after her for me. Marcus offered to help. If you ask me, I'd say he's rather taken with your maid."

"I think you might be right," Aggie said. "He's forever turning up at the house for the most trivial of reasons, when a simple phone call would suffice."

"I wonder why Mr. Barnum had to leave," Mrs. Euston said. "From the build-up you gave him, I feel quite disappointed we never got to meet."

Aggie shrugged. "He rarely stays in the same place for long. Mind you," she added, "he hates public appearances. I wouldn't put it past him to have had one of his minions ring his mobile, just as I went to introduce him, though he seemed genuinely upset by the call. I invited him for dinner tonight, I daresay I'll find out what happened then."

The conversation dried up again. Everyone stared into space.

The surgery doors opened and Doctor Morton came in. He looked tired. "I just finished with the fox." He smiled at Billy. "You called him Razor, right? I found dozens of lacerations, some of them quite deep, but he should recover. Aggie, I checked the park register. They have a vixen and two cubs in the Local Life section. I wonder if we could keep him there after he recovers."

"Of course," Aggie said, "but what about Snowy?"

Doctor Morton's face fell. He wouldn't meet Billy's eye. "Jim's doing everything he can, but we don't carry domestic cat blood here. We requested an emergency supply from town, but it won't get here for at least another hour. There's not much more we can do for him until it arrives."

"Snowy's going to be all right though, isn't he?" Billy's voice shook.

"I honestly don't know." Dr. Morton gave him an apologetic smile. "I better get back in there."

Mrs. Euston put her arm around Billy's shoulders.

196

"Have faith. If anyone can save Snowy, your dad can."

Bitter tears streamed down his face. "You don't understand. This is all my fault. Snowy didn't want to go anywhere near the tunnels, but I talked him into it. If it wasn't for me, he'd be fine."

She pulled him close and together they prepared themselves for a long wait.

Chapter Sixteen
Time to Decide

To Billy, it felt as if entire days had gone by since the batch of Snowy's blood-type had arrived.

His mother looked at her watch. "We really should collect Emma." She saw the look on Billy's face and added, "You stay. Come home with your father."

"Wait for me, Louise," Aggie said. "I'll get someone to give you a lift back to the village."

As soon as they left, Carmen sat beside Billy. "What happened down there?"

"I don't know. Was the gorilla in the room with them, Mr Tinkles?"

"I think so."

Billy stared at the picture of Static-Man on his T-shirt. "I wish my dad would come and tell us what's happening."

The outer door opened and Aggie came back, accompanied by Helen.

"Where's Marcus?" Carmen asked.

"The police asked him to go down to the tunnels to look at the laboratory they discovered next to where they picked up you and Billy." Aggie's voice shook a little as she continued. "The police say someone shot Mr. Tinkles. I don't understand, he was supposed to be on his way to *Benny's Wildlife Center* in Ohio."

"Who would want to shoot a gorilla?" Carmen asked.

Aggie's face hardened. "I don't know, but when I find out who's behind this, they'd better hope the police catch them before I do."

Helen guided her to a chair. "Come on, sit down. I'll get us all a nice cup of tea."

Carmen sat with Aggie.

"Mr. Tinkles was one of the most popular animals we ever had," Aggie said, her eyes glistening with tears. "I remember the day they brought him here. Children adored him. Gorillas usually can't abide eye contact–they see it as a challenge–but he never used to mind when the young ones did it. He just made funny faces at them through the window."

Dr. Euston walked in. His blue surgical scrubs smeared with fresh blood.

Billy jumped to his feet "How is he?"

His father pulled the paper mask from his face. "There were some internal complications. He'd already lost a lot of blood. I couldn't risk another operation until the fresh batch arrived, by then it was too late."

Carmen gasped. Billy flopped back into his chair, stunned. "Snowy's dead?"

His father crouched in front of him. "I'm so sorry. He slipped into a coma a few minutes ago. We're trying to keep him stable, but all the fight's gone out of him. I doubt he'll make it through the night."

"It's all my fault," Billy sobbed. "I killed him."

He felt Aggie's hand on his shoulder. "You mustn't blame yourself. I don't know why Snowy went down those tunnels, but I've known that cat a lot longer than you. He always had a mind of his own. Jim, so long as there's the slightest chance he might recover, I want you to do whatever it takes to keep him alive."

Dr. Euston nodded. He held out his hand to Billy. "Why don't you come on through? You can sit with him until…you know." He put his arm around his son, and together they walked through the surgery doors.

"Good luck," Carmen called after him. She put her head on Aggie's shoulder. "Can we go home now? I want to call my mom."

Snowy woke to the sound of someone whispering in his ear. The voice had a warm familiarity. It called him by his old name. "Roland, wake up Roland. It's time to decide."

"Mom?"

His mother smiled at him, her face calm and gentle. "Of course, dear, who else would it be?"

He sat up and stared around him. They were out in the open, in a field of lush, green grass. A warm breeze teased his whiskers. He sniffed the air. It smelled of fresh apples. "Where am I?"

"You're home, dear."

His mother seemed different somehow, like he saw her through a soft focus lens. "Home? But I live with Bill… Oh, I remember. I'm dead, right?" He cast an anxious glance about him.

"What are you looking for, dear?"

"A headless toad." He ignored his mother's puzzled expression. "Never mind. So, what happens now?"

"That's up to you. You have a choice to make." She stepped aside to reveal a picnic blanket spread out nearby. Dozens of little bowls lined its edges, each one filled with snacks. In the middle of the blanket, five cats rolled around together, in a friendly wrestling match.

"Hey, there's old Todger! I'd recognize those big ears anywhere." He studied the other cats. "There's Bernie, and Reg too, though as I recall, it was usually Reg who had *Bernie* in a headlock."

One of the cats broke away from the group to stand at the edge of the blanket.

Snowy felt a great surge of joy well up inside him. "Missy! Oh, Mom, I can't believe it, everyone's here. Wait, who's the cat holding Todger in a half-nelson?"

His mother sat beside him. "Don't you recognize yourself?"

He looked more closely at the slender, black cat scuffling with his older brother. "If that's me, I've been on a diet."

"It is you, Roland, or it will be, when your time comes."

"What are you talking about? I thought you said I was dead."

"No dear, I said you were home. You can choose to stay, or you can choose to go." She looked over his shoulder.

Snowy followed her gaze. A large bowl appeared on the grass behind them. He couldn't see inside, but it had a familiar odor. "I don't understand."

"Do you remember the river?"

"What?"

"The river, where the human threw you off the bridge."

"Of course I do. I'll never forget it, but what's the

river got to do with all this?"

"Everything, dear," his mother said, in a soothing voice. "You both made a choice that day. You chose to stay, Missy decided to come with me."

"Missy went with you and I stayed? But you weren't even there."

She laughed. "Who do you think pulled you from the water?"

Snowy thought back to the night on the bridge. Missy got thrown first, then the man had dangled the cat box over the edge. He'd tried to hold on, but the insides of the box were too smooth. He'd got angry. 'Stuff it!' He held his breath at the memory of the dark river, rushing toward him. He'd struggled to keep his head out of the freezing water as the current dragged him along.

He remembered grabbing some low branches near the riverbank, but the cold had numbed his limbs. He couldn't pull himself to safety. After a few seconds, he began to lose his grip. Then something touched his paw. It tingled. A dark shape leaned toward him. Then he must have blacked out, because the next thing he knew, he was on the riverbank, coughing up a chest-full of water.

"Mom, how could you possibly know about the river?"

She said nothing, but placed her paw on his.

Snowy jumped. It was exactly the same sensation he'd felt when he'd been hanging on to the branch.

"You were so angry, dear. You wanted revenge. That was your reason to live."

"What about Missy?"

"She was never strong. You know that."

Snowy nodded. "Well, I choose to stay here now. There's nothing for me back there."

"Are you sure? The humans are trying so hard to keep you."

The grass melted away beneath their paws to reveal a hospital room below. Snowy recognized the patient on the table by the wall. "Hey, there's old Razor."

A vet walked underneath him toward another patient. "There's Billy's dad, and look, Mom, the boy himself is in the chair by the bed. He shouldn't slouch across the bed like that. He'll give himself a bad back."

He fell silent when he recognized his own body, lying there, swathed in bandages. Billy looked absolutely shattered.

His mother whispered in his ear. "The human child wants you back."

In the room below, Billy stroked Snowy's paw.

"He's a good kid, Mom. You'd like him, I know you would." He gazed at his brothers and sister. "I don't know what to do. How can I choose?"

"You already have."

He thought for a moment, then nodded. "Will I remember any of this?"

"No, dear, but when the time is right, we'll all be here."

He nuzzled his mother's chin with his head. "Thanks, Mom. How do I get back?"

She gestured to the bowl. "Take a drink."

Snowy trotted over to it. He grinned when he saw the thick plastic straw sticking out of a dark pool of liquid. "Cola. Nice one." He turned back to his mother, but she and the others had already vanished. "So long, guys," he whispered. "It was great to see you again."

The straw expanded as soon as he put his mouth around it. Alarmed, he tried to let go, but his jaws wouldn't open. The straw slid down his throat, choking him. He tried to push it away but his limbs wouldn't obey. He fell to the ground, coughing and spluttering.

"Dad! Dad! Come quick. He's awake. Snowy's awake!"

Snowy opened his eyes to see Billy's face right in front of his own. He tried to speak, but his voice had gone. Someone came up behind him and took a firm, but gentle, grip on his head. He felt a horrible tickling sensation in his throat as Dr. Euston pulled out the breathing tube, then at last he drew a deep, ragged breath.

Billy jumped to his feet, waving his arms in the air. "He's alive! He's alive!"

Dr. Euston joined in.

Doctor Morton came through from the next room. He burst out laughing at the sight of father and son, dancing around the floor. "Nice one, Jim." He checked the monitors at Snowy's bedside. "I can't say I understand how, but it looks like our furry friend here has a good chance of a full recovery." He stroked the side of Snowy's bandaged face. "You are one lucky cat. After that second op, we gave you less than a chance in a thousand of ever coming around."

"Never tell me the odds," Snowy rasped. His throat felt like he'd swallowed a cactus.

Dr. Euston looked at his watch. "He seems to be breathing fine on his own now, son. It's time I got you home. Dr. Morton will keep an eye on Snowy, won't you, David?"

Snowy watched his friend leave, then drifted into a peaceful sleep. He dreamed of green fields and picnic hampers.

The next morning, Billy lay on his bed, reading. He heard raised voices coming from downstairs.

"May I remind you, Madam, we're investigating a crime. We need your son to assist us with our enquiries."

"Inspector Donovan, are you suggesting my son shot that poor gorilla?"

His mother's voice had taken on the same tone she used on him, when she thought he'd said something particularly silly.

"Of course not, but you must understand, this is important."

"My son spent half the night by a sick friend's bedside. He needs to rest. Surely your enquiries can wait until this afternoon."

"No they can't. We're investigating a double homicide. Your son was the first to arrive at the crime scene where the body of Doctor Farofas lay. We believe his death is connected with another murder. We matched the bullets from the crime scene with one we dug out of the gorilla."

When at last she answered, Mrs. Euston voice sounded embarrassed. "I didn't realize. Please, take a seat. I'll fetch my son."

A few minutes later, Billy sat at the kitchen table, answering Inspector Donovan's questions, while a young, plain clothes policeman took notes.

Donovan looked disappointed. "So you didn't see anything, or anybody, on your way through the tunnels."

"No, sir. The security team got there a few seconds after we did. I didn't touch anything, except for Snowy. He was hurt, my dad had to operate on him."

"Who's this Snowy? Make a note, Sergeant, I'll need to interview him too."

"Snowy is the family cat, sir. Found at the crime scene, along with a wild fox. They both received severe injuries."

"Ah." Donovan cleared his throat. "Well, son. Someone changed the wireless frequency on those tunnel cameras. You sure you didn't see anyone else?"

"No one came past us."

"And thank heaven for small mercies," Mrs. Euston said, handing both policemen a cup of tea.

"They could have got in and out via the topside entrances on the outer rim," Billy said. "The nearest one comes out by the elephant area." He noticed the surprised look on Donovan's face. "I...studied the plans for the underground system."

"No use, I'm afraid. Security had all cameras focused on the parade route yesterday afternoon. Any comings and goings through the outer exits went unrecorded." The two policemen stood.

"Am I in trouble," Billy asked, "for taking an electric car without permission?"

"I should think the park has got bigger things to worry about."

His mother showed the policeman out.

"Wow," Billy said, after they'd gone. "A double murder."

His mother frowned at him from the doorway. "It's a dangerous world out there, Billy Euston. You might want to remember that, next time you and Carmen decide to wander off somewhere for a cozy chat."

He didn't correct her. She'd never believe the truth anyway. "Yes, Mom, sorry. Can we call Dad at the park? I want to check on Snowy."

His father wasn't available, but a nurse at the infirmary assured him Snowy had enjoyed a peaceful night.

Dr. Euston came home that evening with good news. "I can't believe the improvement in him," he said. "At this rate, he'll be home before you know it."

Chapter Seventeen
The Return of the Cat

The next morning, Billy waited until he heard his father switch on his electric shaver, then stuck his head around the bathroom door. "Can I come to work with you today? I want to see Snowy."

"Sorry, son. I don't want him to get too excited. What that cat needs more than anything else right now, is rest and a healthy diet."

Billy pulled a face. "Can I at least pack some food for him."

"Your mother already did. And before you ask, no, there weren't any crispy snacks, bottles of cola, or Custard Creams included. Snowy needs a balanced eating plan. I don't think you realize how close we came to losing him." His face softened. "Tell you what, maybe your mom can bring you and Emma for a quick visit tomorrow."

Just after lunch, Carmen came over. Billy could see she was bursting to tell him something. They hurried to his room. She threw her pink cycle helmet on the bed. "You'll never guess what's happened."

"I bet I can. The police interviewed you. Fur-Face, I mean, Professor Farofas, is dead. That must have been his shoe you saw in the lab."

"Wrong," she said, with a triumphant smile. "They

want to question Benedict Barnum."

"Whatever for?"

"My thoughts exactly." Carmen sat at the desk. "That Inspector Donovan came round again this morning. I knew it must be about something important, so I hung around outside the door to listen. From what I could make out, Farofas developed brain implants which let him control animals. He put the prototype in Razor's head. Your dad did a CAT scan and found it, but he can't remove the chip without killing Razor."

"Wow," Billy said. "Poor Razor. But of course, it wasn't the prototype. That must be the one in Snowy. He's had his since last Christmas."

"They didn't mention Snowy. They wanted to know how Farofas and Gladstone had access to the park underground for all this time. Aggie got really mad. She thought they suspected her." Carmen sat up, looking pleased with herself. "That's when I barged in and told him not to be so silly."

Billy grinned. "Good for you, but I still don't understand why they want to talk to Barnum."

"I was getting to that. I said Aggie would never hurt any animal. Inspector Donovan just looked at me like I was crazy or something, then he showed us an evidence bag with a squashed cigar end in it. He said they found it in the viewing room where Snowy got hurt. Apparently, you can't buy that brand in England. Aggie said they should try asking Bennie, because he owns a plantation, and knows all about cigars. The Inspector said they'd already gone to his hotel, but he'd flown back to the States in his private jet. I think they suspect he's involved."

Billy sat on his bed, taking it all in.

"It doesn't make sense," Carmen said. "Bennie can't have been there. He was at the presentation with Aggie, remember? Besides, he seems so nice."

"I haven't met him," Billy said, "but being nice could be just an act, or maybe he's kind to humans but not animals. Anyway, Farofas couldn't have done all this alone."

"Well, I wouldn't like to be in Bennie's shoes if my gran finds out he's involved."

The bedroom door opened and Emma toddled into the room, demanding a piggyback ride. Billy let her clamber onto his back while they all went downstairs for ice cream.

Dr. Euston came home just after lunch. He dropped a newspaper on the kitchen table, where Carmen and Billy helped Emma draw pictures of Snowy.

The headline read:

MURDER AT ADVENTURE SAFARI!

Dr. Euston took a swig from Billy's bottle of cola. "The park was crawling with reporters and camera crews this morning. They even caught a TV crew trying to sneak into the restricted area where Farofas died."

"Vultures," Carmen said. "Why didn't security turn them away at the entrance?"

Dr. Euston laughed. "You looked just like Aggie then. Unfortunately, there's this little thing we have called 'freedom of the press', so we had to grin and bear it. I suppose we should expect a few days under the spotlight, considering what happened."

That night, the Eustons watched the TV news, but

only the local independent channel covered the death at *Adventure Safari*.

"There's Donovan," Billy said, when the policeman appeared on the screen.

Someone held a large microphone under the inspector's chin as he made a brief statement. "We have concluded our preliminary investigation. Doctor Farofas was the victim of an unfortunate and tragic accident."

The Eustons gaped in collective disbelief.

The news reporter asked a question. "Is it true the park's security team discovered the remains of Dr. Farofas alongside the escaped gorilla which killed him?"

"We discovered several animals with the deceased, including a gorilla. We believe the doctor was working alone with them when the gorilla became agitated and attacked him."

"Inspector, surely gorillas are placid creatures."

"Normally, yes. However, we believe he provoked the animal by inadvertently looking it in the eye. According to our expert, gorillas see eye contact as a challenge to their authority. This was a terrible accident. The animal in question was humanely put down. The park's owner has agreed to review all safety procedures. Our investigation is now closed."

The TV camera turned on the female reporter. "A good man, devoted to his work, suffers a horrible death. Killed by one of the very animals he sought to help. Doctor Farofas had no living relatives, but will be greatly missed by all who work here. Tina Thomas, reporting from *Adventure Safari*. Now, back to the studio."

"What's going on?" Billy's mother almost shouted.

"Yesterday, Inspector Donovan said there'd been a double murder. Now he says it was an accident?"

"This can't be right," Billy said. "Farofas didn't work for the park. Aggie fired him ages ago."

Just then, the doorbell rang. His father went to answer it.

Billy and his mother sat in silence, too shocked to speak.

Dr. Euston came back into the room, closely followed by a smart dressed man in a black suit and tie. The stranger held up an identity card. Billy just had time to make out a picture of a winged horse, before the man whisked it away.

"Sorry to trouble you at home, but I have a very important matter to discuss with you. My name is Anderson, I work for the British secret service."

A few minutes later, Anderson left.

The phone rang. Dr. Euston went out into the hall to answer it. "Oh, hello Aggie… Yes they've been here too… No, I don't understand either. I suppose, if it's a matter of national security… No, me neither… What? They couldn't, could they? Right, okay then. In that case, it never happened… Me too."

Dr. Euston came back into the room. "That was Aggie, she's had a visit too. Apparently, whatever Farofas was up to has to be hushed up. We all have to stick to the story about Mr. Tinkles escaping."

Billy jumped to his feet. "But that's a lie. They're making Farofas out to be some kind of hero."

"I know," Dr. Euston said, "but Aggie's says if the truth leaks out, M.I.5. threatened to shut down *Adventure Safari* while they investigate. They've said they'd make sure it never opened again."

Billy's mother put her hand to her mouth. "Could they really do that?"

"Aggie seems to think so. She said the man who came to see her had worked with her father. He was really embarrassed about it all, but she believed him."

"Do you think they'll take Razor and Snowy away?" Billy asked, suddenly worried.

His father looked at him in surprise. "I shouldn't think so, why?"

"The Secret Service might want to question them."

"I don't understand. How could they question them?"

"You know," Billy said, "the microchips in their brains."

"Right, very funny. The implants don't make an animal talk. They enhance reception in a normally unused area of the brain, allowing the animal to receive signals from a remote device. Mind you, we should probably increase security around the fox enclosure, in case someone decides they want Razor's chip."

"What about Snowy?"

"Snowy? He doesn't have an implant."

Now it was Billy's turn to look surprised. "Are you sure?"

"Of course. As soon as Marcus told me what he'd found in the lab. I ran C.A.T. scans on all three animals, Only Razor had a microchip in his brain."

Billy felt lightheaded. "But Snowy's got all those scars behind his ear. I saw them."

"I know," Dr. Euston said. "I daresay he got them when he got run over last winter. Aggie made Professor

Farofas patch him up, but that's all he did." He noticed the look on his son's face. "Believe me, Bill, there's nothing in Snowy's head which doesn't belong there."

At *Adventure Safari* the following afternoon, Mrs. Euston took Emma for an ice cream while Billy followed Doctor Morton through to the recovery room to visit Snowy. He let out a horrified gasp when he saw his friend.

"He's in a lot better shape than he looks. We had to shave off most of his fur before your father could start work on him."

Snowy lay curled up in a large, comfortable-looking basket in the corner of the room. After three days, his fur had just started to grow back. He'd lost a lot of weight, and the lack of fur made him look even smaller.

"How long before you take those stitches out?"

"We don't have to," Dr. Morton said. "They'll dissolve over the next few weeks. By the time his fur grows back, he'll be as good as new.

"You hear that?" Billy crouched beside the cat basket. "You're going to be just fine."

Doctor Morton went back to his desk, in the next room.

Snowy opened his eyes. He looked exhausted. "Easy for you to say." He struggled to sit up. "Where's me bag of grapes then?"

"Sorry," Billy said. "Dad gave strict orders. I can't give you anything, but when you come home, I promise we'll have a massive feast to celebrate."

"Can't be helped, I suppose. How are the others doing?"

Billy wanted to pick up Snowy and cuddle him, but

Doctor Morton had warned against it, so he settled for stroking Snowy's bald head. "Razor's doing fine, but I'm afraid Mr. Tinkles didn't make it. Aggie's holding a burial service for him on Friday."

Snowy examined his shaved paws. "Pity. I liked him. Did they get the bad guys?"

"Only Farofas. He's dead. The Secret Service wants the whole thing hushed up, so even if they catch the others, I don't suppose we'll ever know."

Snowy flopped back on the cushion. "I'm not surprised. Making animals talk is a big deal. I don't think humans are ready for it."

Billy sat on the floor with his back against the wall. "About that."

When he'd finished explaining, Snowy looked thoughtful for a while. "I don't have an implant then?"

"No."

"And even if I did, it wouldn't make me talk."

"Not according to Marcus and my dad."

"So you're saying, by some freak of nature, I can speak human, but only *you* can understand me, right?"

"It must have been the car accident." Billy said.

Snowy grinned. "Cool. Wait, what about old Tin-head? If his implant has nothing to do with actually talking, how come you can understand him?"

"I don't know. Maybe it's a combination of the chip and the helmet. Doctor Morton says they plan to put him in with Scala and the cubs tomorrow."

Snowy went to sit up, then seemed to think better of it. "Well, we said we'd find his family and we did. Maybe we should go into business, you know: 'Snowy and Billy–Animal Detectives'.

Doctor Morton tapped on the surgery door. "Sorry, time's up."

"Okay, thanks." Billy placed his hand on Snowy's head, then got ready to leave. When he reached the door, he looked back over his shoulder. "I think 'Billy and Snowy' has a much better ring to it. See you soon…partner."

The following day, Billy's friend Patrick arrived from London with his parents for a visit. Billy's father took the day off work and after lunch, Aggie brought Carmen around. They spent the afternoon at *Adventure Safari*. Afterwards, they enjoyed a thirty-minute water pistol fight in the Eustons' back yard. Aggie got disqualified for using the six-pint Thunder Cannon she'd brought in from her Land Rover. Then it was time to set up the barbecue.

Later, Billy lay on his bed, with his hands behind his head, listening to the creaking sound of Patrick's camp bed, by the far wall.

After a while, Patrick sat up. "I can't sleep. It's too quiet. I'm glad you like it, but I could never get used to living out here in Little Jamberry, or whatever they call this place."

Billy didn't answer for a moment. A contented smile spread across his face as he conjured up a mental picture of the weathered, good-natured faces of the locals. They'd all made him feel welcome, like he mattered in some way. In London, people always seemed in such a hurry. "Actually, it's Little Chumberry," he said, "but I prefer to call it 'home'."

Patrick grinned. "Of course you do. I saw the way

you chatted with Carmen, but you said she's seeing that Jean-Pierre bloke in Paris. I hate to say it, mate, but she'll soon forget you when she goes back to France."

Billy liked Carmen, but she seemed to think of him as an honorary brother. Still, if Patrick thought they were an item, he didn't want to spoil his new reputation as a ladies' man. Besides, Carmen may have Jean-Pierre's picture in her locket, but she'd never met the man. Snowy had told him all about his friend's crush on the French TV star. "We'll see," he said. "We'll see."

Another three weeks passed before Dr. Euston carried Snowy through the front door. He looked a hundred times better than when Billy had seen him after his surgery, though his black hair had another month of growing to do before his coat regained its former glory. As promised, the family held a homecoming feast in his honor.

Billy had to wait until his parents went to put Emma to bed before he could speak to his friend properly. "How do you feel?"

The cat pushed Emma's bendy straw into the top of a cola bottle. "I feel…good." He took a long slurp.

Billy stroked his head. "We have to be extra careful. If my parents catch me talking to you again, they'll send me to an insane asylum for sure."

"That might not be so easy."

"I know, I know. But I don't want them thinking I've gone crazy. What?"

Snowy stared past him.

Billy whirled around to see his parents, watching him from halfway up the stairs. His mother had her hand over her mouth–she looked about to cry.

"Mom! Dad! I can explain. I…er…"

Snowy's whiskers sagged. "Give it up, Bill." He climbed off the couch, wincing when his injured hind leg hit the carpet. "Sit 'em down at the kitchen table while I get the cards. You fetch the Monopoly set."

The color drained from Billy's cheeks. "What about you?"

"We'll just have to trust them to keep a secret."

"I'm so sorry."

"Don't be, you couldn't help it." Snowy hobbled across the floor toward the hall. In the doorway, he looked back over his shoulder with an impish grin. "After all, you're only human."

THE END

Born in England, Jon Gibbs now lives in the USA with his wife and three children. Founder of the New Jersey Authors' Network (http://www.njauthorsnetwork.com) and FindAWritingGroup.com, he can usually be found hunched over the computer in his basement office. One day he hopes to figure out how to switch it on.

To find out more about Snowy, and Jon's other writing, visit www.acatofninetales.com or drop by Jon's online journal.

An Englishman in New Jersey
http://jongibbs.livejournal.com